KAREN ROMANO YOUNG

Video

GREENWILLOW BOOKS, NEW YORK

Grateful acknowledgment is made to the following
for permission to quote from copyrighted material:

From "Don't Play with Bruno" by John Forster and Tom Chapin,
© 1989 Limousine Music Co. and The Last Music Co. (ASCAP), from Tom Chapin's
Moonboat recording. Used with permission. All rights reserved.

From "The Woman at the Washington Zoo" by Randall Jarrell,
© 1960 by Randall Jarrell, reprinted in The Complete Poems of Randall Jarrell,
Farrar, Straus & Giroux, 1989. Permission granted by Rhoda Weyr Agency, New York.

The text of this book is set in Times Roman Italic,
Baskerville, and Optima.

Printed in the United States of America
First Edition
10 9 8 7 6 5 4 3 2 1

Library of Congress Cataloging-in-Publication Data
Young, Karen Romano.
    Video / Karen Romano Young.
        p.   cm.
    Summary: "Mean Janine" turns out to be a complicated person, as Eric discovers dur-
ing his spring term assignment to observe a classmate and record his observations, an assignment that changes both of them in unexpected ways.
    ISBN 0-688-16517-6
    [1. Schools—Fiction.   2. Interpersonal relations—Fiction.   3. Family life—Fiction.
4. Wetlands—Fiction.]
    I. Title.   PZ7.Y8665Vi   1999
    [Fic]—dc21   98-32208   CIP   AC

For Peg and Kim, with love,

and to Annie

You can observe a lot by watching.
  —YOGI BERRA

You know what I was,
You see what I am: change me, change me!
  —RANDALL JARRELL

Don't play with Bruno. Bruno is a dweeb.
A dweeb? What's a dweeb?
Oh, you know. Like Bruno.
  —JOHN FORSTER AND TOM CHAPIN

Chapter 1

The man is as tall, dark, and handsome as any girl's dream, his hair under the cloudy sky agleam like the water at his feet.

I'm too young for this, Janine thinks, too young to be caught under such a spell.

He drives his fishing pole into the sand and brushes off both hands on his blue T-shirt. He loves the warm air, stretches his arms up into it. He smooths the shirt over his chest, down, down, and as his hands move lower, he looks at Janine at last. The corners of his mouth turn up, but his expression is hardly what anyone smart would call a smile.

I'm too young, she thinks again. Get me away from him.

Her feet turn against her and walk toward him. Get me away.

His hands move so casually over his stomach and his hips.

Get him away from me!

☙ *Janine*

If you ask me, it all began the second week of spring term, when Mr. Mitchell Lincoln first put those green marble notebooks in our hands. I'm a *G*, so my turn—and my notebook—came on the first day of what he called interviews.

Lincoln pulled up a chair, sat his fat self down on it backward, and looked into my face. I moved back a few inches.

"So!" he announced. "This is the assignment: You are to choose a real person, an interesting person, to observe for the spring term."

Unreal. I couldn't believe this was happening. "What happened to the friendship project my brother and sister did?" My voice sounded loud in the empty classroom.

I'd waited all my life to get to eighth grade, make honors fall term, and take Whole Learning with Lincoln, and now look! He'd come up with this lame new assignment. Well, if I couldn't do the famous friendship project with Artie O'Halloran, my heart's desire and destiny, I didn't want to do anything at all.

Mr. Lincoln just shrugged. "Change is good," he said. How stupid! Because of the friendship project, romances had blossomed, battles had raged, newspaper articles had been published ("Interpersonal Relationships Under the Eye of Marsh Park Students"). Who needed change?

"Who interests you, Janine?" he asked. He rested his elbows on the back of his chair and wove his fingers together and looked into my eyes. He had a turquoise ring in a thunderbird shape on his left ring finger. His hair and mustache were graying brown, and his brown eyes had little wrinkles around the corners. Getting old.

"Artie O'Halloran?" I suggested.

"Oh. I'm afraid he's already—somebody's already observing him."

I collapsed against the seat back and ran through the alphabet up to *G*. Who else might have picked Artie before I got my alphabetical chance? Cynthia Dankowitz? Barbara Finney? Or one of those other boy-crazy dweebs?

"Anybody else interest you?"

I shrugged, disgusted. Somebody else was going to be observing Artie's white-blond hair, his blue, blue eyes.

"What about your family, for example?"

I made a gagging noise. "Like who, my mother?" I gave him the rundown on her. "She runs a catering business from home, Yvonne's. She's a Cordon Bleu cook. And she has her master's in business administration."

"Uh-huh. Where is she at this precise moment, this woman you know so well?" He pressed a finger to his temple as if it would help me think. I closed my eyes to keep from watching him and tried to picture my mother.

"She's sitting at her little French desk, drinking her little French cup of coffee, and ordering the food for her dinner party. Minding her own business." I paused for effect. He showed no response.

"Continue," he said.

"About my family? Well, there's Julia. You know her." I let my voice grow even more bored. "She's a senior, editor of the high school paper, *The Fox*. She won an award for her editorial, remember? 'Why High School Students Should Have the Right to Vote.' " I waved my hand as if there were smoke in the room.

"What's she *like* these days?"

"She's into organic food—herbs and vegetables with no pesticides. And boys are always calling her." I bobbed my eyebrows up and down.

3

"Calling for what, herbs?"

Bonehead. "Calling for dates!"

"Organic ones?"

I frowned and said nothing.

"Ah," he said. "And my friend Jeff?"

"Well, you just *had* Jeff last year. I can't do him."

"Because I had him?"

"He's in love with himself already. His brain's still as small as his hockey puck." Mr. Lincoln's eyes finally showed that flicker of annoyance I'm so used to seeing in adults. He looked at his watch. But when he spoke, his voice was gentle and level.

"Okay, Janine. Then whom do you have in mind?"

"My father's completely unavailable. He's a builder, and he practically lives at work. You can't make me do *him*—"

I was embarrassed enough by Daddy without having to observe him, to watch closely as he told silly stories and ridiculous sayings to everyone he met. Julia was big on sayings, too, but at least hers made sense; they weren't things like "I did it in one swell foop! I mean one smell poop! I mean fast, wow." I shuddered at the idea that I had ever thought Daddy was funny.

"I'm not making you—"

"And how could I choose from people in school? They're all such dweebs!"

"Dweebs?" he echoed in his calmest tone. "Well, which of your friends do you consider most popular?"

I thought. I refused to embarrass myself by mentioning Artie again.

Barbara Finney? Since she'd become a Marsh Park Middle School cheerleader, her big mouth had gotten even bigger.

Susan Hackman. She just wanted to hang around Barbara.

4

Quiet, pretty, loyal, single-minded. Always painting rocks or something. Curly blond hair and little hands. Not someone you'd expect to find cheerleading, but that's what she was doing. Boring.

Kelly Kim? It's boys who liked her, not girls, and not just because she was always laughing, just because of her gigantic—

"Apart from me?" I asked.

"You're the most popular?"

"I suppose so."

"Including the boys?"

Boys! I hardly counted them, though Julia said I'd start to soon, now that dancing school was about to start that spring. If it weren't for kickball and baseball, I'd avoid them completely. I shook my head. "John Heinz, maybe, but they just like him because he tells jokes. That's not popularity."

"What is?" He leaned forward as though this were a key question. "Saving the world? Being a business success? Being a star hockey player?"

"It's being able to get people to do what you want," I said without hesitation. "It's having them agree with you."

"And that's why you're most popular, Janine?"

I nodded.

"Everybody wants to be on my team when we play kickball," I said. "They play by my rules, too, the ones Artie and I made up." There were more pieces of proof, if Lincoln needed them: how everyone always moved aside to give me a seat at the popular table in the cafeteria, how they let me have the number 1 shirt when we played fall soccer, how I got the best Secret Santa gifts in the class: musical socks, Russell Stover Santas, and a snow globe of a skater on a pond. If that wasn't popularity, I didn't know what was.

"So they play by your rules?" Lincoln repeated.

"And Artie's," I said, not wanting to seem too full of myself, as my mother would say.

"And you're the most interesting person you know?"

"I guess I am." All of a sudden I felt a little off center. The trouble was that everything seemed to have changed this winter. The things that I was interested in—kickball and science and saving the wetlands—seemed like jokes to Barbara, Susan, and Kelly. And their ideas of how to spend their lives—practicing cow jumps and cheers and reading *Seventeen*—made me practically retch. I hoped it was a phase, something my mother is always saying Julia is going through. At least if I studied myself, I wouldn't be forced to pay attention to anything dweebish. I just didn't want to know more about cheerleading than I'd already picked up, thank you very much.

"Fine!" Mr. Lincoln said. He made a note and shut his book. Then he handed me a green marble-cover notebook. "You'll use this for your illustrations. I'll be reading it over once a week. Study yourself, until you find someone who interests you more."

At the top of the first page of the notebook, I wrote my name large in my best handwriting, in pen.

Janine Marguerite Gagnon

◗ *Eric*

I would never have gotten stuck at Janine Gagnon's own personal bus stop if it hadn't been for Mr. Lincoln, my new science teacher. Excuse me. It's not science; it's Whole Learning, which allegedly includes science, English, foreign language, and social studies. Art, gym, and math are separate. I found this out when I came in last week to meet the principal and get shown around. Since Mr. Lincoln is going to be teaching me almost every subject, I wanted to introduce myself. He told me about this observation project, and I knew right away that it was trouble.

But I guess he didn't seriously consider my objections after all. "The most important thing you can get out of school is the skill of observation," Mr. Lincoln said. Well, after eight and a half years at the Haycock School, first as a day student and, since I was ten, as a boarder, my scientific skills were more than up to the standards of a public middle school.

"I've already learned all I need to know about observation," I had told him then.

"Oh?" He twisted his dark brown mustache and looked at me steadily.

"Do you want to know what the weather's going to be tomorrow? What phase of the moon we're in? The crop outlook for the spring?"

I was determined to make a good impression. Even if I did have to spend a term in public school, against my will, I still intended to go to an excellent college, and I needed my usual A in science.

When he didn't respond, I went on. "I'm planning to go into meteorology, you know. Today I've already observed the sky, the light, the cloud cover, the dew point, the barometric pressure. I've got the moon on video every night for the last week."

"The moon on *video?*"

"Sure!" I said some Latin to him then. "*Veni, vidi, video.*"

He didn't react. I translated: "I came, I saw, I videoed. It's a great way to record things."

Lincoln nodded. "We're going to observe people, Eric," he said. "Lots more interesting than things."

I realized I'd do better with him by showing I was willing to learn than by showing off what I already knew. "I think it should be a girl," I said. "I've been going to an all-male school, you know, and I haven't had many chances to observe females."

Mr. Lincoln's eyebrows went up and down. "Anyone specific?"

My stomach flip-flopped. At Haycock I had been so busy dreaming of women that I'd never thought what it would be like to be around girls. I was too embarrassed to name any of the real standouts: not Barbara Finney, with those long chestnut braids (one red ribbon, one white, Marsh Park Middle School colors). Not her blond curly-top best friend Susan, with that sweet way about her and the paint box stuck in the back of her binder. Not Kelly Kim, with her pretty Asian hair, corny elephant jokes, and those incredible big—

To avoid certain personal disaster, I forced my brain to change direction: Marcy Moreno, a girl who rode the bus with me and was in Whole Learning with the rest of the eighth-grade honors kids. No. She was brown colored (my mom would say black, but that's not accurate), with brown hair and plain brown eyes and even a brown coat, and all she'd done since we started the term was stand off to one side, reading through all the Madeleine L'Engle books, one after the other. She didn't talk to anybody. No, Marcy just was not interesting enough to keep my attention all term long, nowhere close.

Mr. Lincoln sat waiting, his arms on the back of his chair (he rides it backward in his cowboy boots, yee-ha). I realized

I was counting girls on my fingers. I reached my thumb and sat holding it, my mind blank.

He ran his fingers over the names in his planner. His finger stopped. "Janine Gagnon?" he suggested.

I lifted my shoulders and let them drop. "Couldn't I do my sister?" I asked desperately. But I knew I really didn't want to study little seven-year-old Katie, didn't want to see any closer how sad and confused she'd been since Dad left.

Janine Gagnon was the reason Katie insisted on going to the Henry Street bus stop, and that meant Mom had to drive us because I couldn't walk around the corner with my broken leg. Katie was afraid of Janine, whom she called Mean Janine, on account of stories she'd heard from her best friend, Amy Panucci, who in turn had heard them from her brothers, Charlie, another Whole Learner, and Anthony, a fifth grader. But even Janine—that bratty little boss of the block whom I'd been able to avoid by going to private school all these years— would be better than Katie.

I still wonder why I told Mr. Lincoln yes. I guess you'd say it was a weak moment. It had more to do with feeling like a stranger in my own house, now that I'd been dragged home from Haycock, than being a new kid in public school. It had a lot to do with trying to get along with a guy I'd be spending more time with in the next couple of months than I'd ever spent with my own father. It also had a lot to do with my mobility. It was rough walking on crutches with a cast from my toes to my thigh, and all the snow we'd had lately just added to the confusion.

"Just don't let her know," I said wearily.

"Oh, no," he said. "That's one of the rules. This project is purely scientific. Your job is not to judge but to see."

"Can I video her?" It was a new idea. So far a person had never been the subject of one of my videos.

He looked me firmly in the eye. "The idea is to observe, not spy, Eric. We'll have no crimes against privacy. Janine is a person, not a weather sign, not a thing."

Well, that remained to be seen. I'd been sitting behind Janine in Whole Learning for a week now and had noticed only that she was the kind of person who dumped papers over her shoulder instead of turning around to pass them.

I didn't really see the difference between observing people and spying on them, but I said, "I'm not going to look in her windows or anything. It's just not that easy for me to get around right now. With a camera I can zoom in from a distance."

He gave me an observation notebook then. It was a cheap plain green marbled one from Wal-Mart, nothing you'd ever see at Haycock. I turned to the first page and wrote her name small and scrawly, in pencil, so no one could read it over my shoulder no matter how hard he squinted.

Janine Gagnon

JANINE

SCIENCE OBSERVATION

JANUARY 25

My hair is golden brown and cut to my chin in a classic pageboy (on my mother's instructions to Peter, the faggy hairdresser). I have her hair; at least it's the color hers was before she went frosty. Jeff and Julia got my father's looks: blue eyes and wavy dark brown hair. I've tried to grow mine as long as Julia's, but it doesn't grow past my shoulders. Her fat braid goes to the middle of her back. Lucky. But I have the luck when it comes to eyes; mine are spicy brown.

I'm very athletic. I'm the best around at soccer and baseball and tennis. When I was in sixth grade, I started the Kickball Club. It was at recess. If you didn't play kickball, you couldn't be in the club. Ever since then I've been the star of the class. I'm small, and I'm wiry. And I'm good. I'm the best of the girls, and Artie O'Halloran is the best of the boys.

Not as many people play kickball as last year. Now that we're in eighth grade, there isn't much of a recess, just ten minutes of hanging-around time after lunch. If they'd all hurry up and eat and quit talking, we could get a couple of innings in. Last summer at Park and Rec I hit .415 in softball, more than Artie. And I'm even better at kickball. Short recess or not, I've still got that star quality.

Clothes help. I wear a lot of yellow, and my shoes are usually loafers or Adidas soccer sneakers, except for on snow days like today. Then I'm stuck wearing Jeff's old hiking boots, which have the shape of his bony feet, not mine. I hate them! I like to look put-together, and these boots don't suit me at all. Jeff says they make me look even more like a boy than usual. Julia says that isn't true, but they're not that bad, even kind of funky, so I shouldn't make such a fuss. My father says I'll have to cope, what with the construction business in the shape it's in. My mother says when I get taller (she's more hopeful than I am), my feet will grow.

It's not fair. My parents can't be telling the truth about their finances. They have plenty of money. They're just cheap! All my life, for example, I've been begging, pleading, praying for a dog or a cat or a bird or anything alive that doesn't have green leaves. And why is the answer always no? Allergies? Money? No. My mother says animals are dirty (she means *disgusting*) and my dad lets her think it. It's her house, he says. It's unbelievable.

But enough about them. This is supposed to be about me. I live in a yellow house with a green front door and a red mailbox. It's as nice as the other houses on Kingfisher Lane—even nicer!—because my father built it himself in this new development that borders on the wetlands.

Our house is the one with the little brass horn with pinecones and a red ribbon on the door, left over from Christmas. Julia wanted to hang a cardboard Hallmark Cupid for Valentine's Day, but Mother said it was tacky. But Julia says, when it comes to Valentine's Day, tacky is good. Mother says Julia has an answer for everything. Usually the wrong one, I'd say.

▶ *Eric*

It wasn't surprising that it had snowed in upstate New York during winter vacation, right on target for the latitude and elevation there. The last thing I had expected, when we drove home from the mountains three days earlier than we'd planned, was that the snow would still be on the ground all the way south to Marsh Park.

We hadn't come back early just because of my accident. No, it was my parents. For more than a year they'd been fighting over money and jobs, getting nastier as time went on. The basic problem, it seemed to me, was that my mother wanted to go back to school and get a job, and my father wanted her to join a women's club and plant flowers. My mother says it went much deeper than that, but that was the point the argument always swung on. Our ski trip was supposed to be an opportunity for the family to be together and "do some healing." Mom's words.

It seemed that Dad had assigned everybody in our family a job. Dad was the boss, the big moneymaker. Mom was the helper, the cleaner, the giver who was just supposed to take care of everybody, in and out of our family. Katie was supposed to be sweet, quiet, and beautiful. Beautiful was no problem, but sweet came and went, and quiet was just plain impossible. By the time you're in first grade, I guess, there's more to life than just being adorable. All this, of course, was Mom's version. The only thing Dad ever talked to me about was my role.

I was supposed to be the family genius. My father had often told me that all his hopes hung on me. He'd gotten into Haycock on a scholarship, but he was able to pay for me. He'd had to scrape and save to go to Dartmouth, but with his

Wall Street salary I would be able to choose my college. It was up to me to know how to do things and to do them well. And this year's activity was skiing. *Was*, I said. Because for me skiing was a thing of the past.

It was not exactly the most ingenious thing to do to try an advanced slope on my fifth day of skiing. But when Dad suggested it, I had been skiing just well enough to try. There was no ball involved in skiing, for one thing. For me that was a big plus. Maybe, just maybe, it was a sport I could excel at. Hope made me take a chance. I saw the black diamond on the top of that hill—I should say *cliff*—and I got puffed up full of more confidence than I'd ever felt in regular life. I could already imagine myself zipping and bobbing up and down the moguls, digging my sharp edges into their icy sides. I imagined Dad's pride afterward when he'd brag about me in the lodge to Mom and Katie. So when my father said, "Think you can handle it, Ric?"—that name that only he called me—there was only one right answer.

I'm not exactly sure what took place in the emergency room while I was being rushed in, knocked out, and patched up. I only know that by the time my leg was set and plastered, my father was well down the Taconic Parkway to New York City in our BMW, and Mom, Katie, and I were headed east on Route 90 in a rental car.

Mom said the rental car was for me, because it had more room for my leg. It wasn't until I was settled across the backseat and Katie was in the front and Mom was driving, until I'd finished checking the condition of my video camera (which had been in my backpack when I fell going down the advanced slope "Dipsy Doodle," and which, thank God, was all right) that I realized we weren't going back to the lodge to meet Dad.

When I asked about Dad, I got a tight-lipped "He won't be coming home, Eric," from Mom. Dad thinks *Ric* sounds stronger than *Eric*. I was feeling anything but strong at the moment.

"Not ever?" asked Katie.

Mom gave no answer, not even tears.

It seemed as if that accident had made him give up hope on all of us: too-opinionated Mom, smart but athletically disappointing me, and even beautiful but not sweet or quiet, perfectly excellent Katie. He was gone.

Now I overheard calm, measured phone conversations with lawyers and hushed, nasty conversations with Dad. Katie and I were not allowed to see him. That was not the first ruling Mom had made, though. The first thing she had done after that unlucky skiing trip was to phone Haycock and tell them I wouldn't be coming back. Then she broke it to me.

"I want you home," Mom said. There was a quaver in her voice, but her blue-green eyes were completely steady.

I think that the first time in someone's life that she puts her foot down is probably the time that she puts it down the hardest. I went berserk. I yelled and argued and talked and reasoned. But she would not be moved. When Pete Hotchkiss, my roommate, called to see where I was, she told him I would not be back before I could get hold of the phone. I told her, and Dad phoned her and faxed her and left messages for her, that we would take it one term at a time. She didn't answer me. And she changed the telephone number on him.

JANINE

SCIENCE OBSERVATION
FEBRUARY 7

Choose a quote from the list on the board and comment on it, keeping your subject in mind.
"You're known by the company you keep."

Barbara Finney, Susan Hackman, and Kelly Kim have been in the Kickball Club since the first day I started it, back in sixth grade. So I guess they're known by being kickball players like me.

Barbara kicks a mean kickball. She cheers for anything that moves, even the dweebs who kick pop flies and get out, which is annoying. It's also annoying that she's started being a cheerleader for real and practices it sometimes when I need her to play kickball. If I get to choose first, I naturally choose Barbara.

Susan is good to have on your team because she's a fast runner and nervy. She's hardly ever on my team, though, because Artie always takes her for his first pick of the girls.

Kelly Kim used to be a better player but slow. Now she is mostly just slow, which is a pain when you only have ten minutes to play and it's not like everybody gets a lot of ups. The last time I got stuck with her on my team, I told her to get a move on. She just laughed and said something behind her hand to Barbara. As Julia would say, you have to endure what you can't cure. So I have to put up with Kelly.

Barbara, Susan, Kelly, and I have been friends since kindergarten. All together we are the popular group, and everyone wants to be with us and be like us. Why wouldn't they? We will probably stay best friends until the end of high school. After that, who knows?

▶ *Eric*

A few days after Mr. Lincoln finished interviewing the whole Whole Learning class in alphabetical order, Charlie Panucci got behind me in the lunch line and asked me who I had to observe. Well, rule number one was that we were supposed to keep that information private, and I was planning to follow that rule as a matter of self-preservation. All I could think of was how to keep Charlie talking to me without giving away the fact that my subject was Janine. I admit I got a bit overdramatic.

"Well, it's one of *them*, that's for sure," I said, bobbing my eyebrows at him.

He grinned. "Oh, yeah? Anyone special?"

I rolled my eyes at the ceiling and acted mysterious.

"I bet it's Kelly," he said.

"Yeah, sure," I said.

"Cynthia?"

"Yeah, right," I said. It went on like that for a while.

17

Panucci was a tall guy who walked like Pete Hotchkiss, my roommate at Haycock and the captain of the Junior Varsity lacrosse team: on the balls of his feet. Charlie shot baskets at recess, and once when Mom and I picked Katie up from Amy's, he and Anthony were outside on Rollerblades, which my father would have said were girly.

Not only had I been at Haycock every school year, but in summer I went to sleep-away camp. I didn't know Charlie. And Charlie didn't know that I couldn't shoot a basket or roller-skate to save my life, whether or not this cast was on my leg. Well, there wasn't any way he was going to find out, so I acted up a storm.

I said vaguely, "Someone worth looking at." Yeah, in a shooting gallery. I slid my tray along the rail and picked up a hot dog and extra macaroni and cheese.

He laughed. "Lucky you." If only he knew. He loaded his hot dog with sauerkraut and took two salads.

"How about you?" I asked, to change the subject. "Someone soft and cuddly?" If anything would get him guessing anyone but Janine, that would.

He shook his head in a way that made me wish I had curly hair as well as a lot more height. "No such luck," he said, and acted mysterious to get me back.

Now my broken leg gave me a break because Charlie carried my tray to a table (something I can't do on crutches) without being asked and sat down with me. Then other guys came, easily, just like that, because of Charlie.

It would have been a good day except for Janine.

Whatever had possessed me to say I'd observe her? There was too much riding on my Whole Learning grade to keep on avoiding the observation project. But I was sorrier than ever that I'd agreed to watch Janine. My stomach was in enough of a nervous state as it was. And there were so many finer things—females, I should say—in life.

I looked at the plaster cast on my foot, which bore Janine's signature in fat green marker on my heel. She had written her name big, right over the edge of a cat Susan Hackman had just finished drawing. Susan had been sketching the cat, sitting in her seat behind mine, while I sat backward in my chair studying my Wordly Wise book at her desk. It had been a cozy moment until Janine tapped my back and held up her green marker.

"Anyplace special?" she'd asked, and when I shook my head, she signed as if she wanted to push Susan and her cat right off the cast.

At least I didn't have to go far to observe Janine. She was right outside every morning at the bus stop, where she waited all alone in plain earshot of what sounded like a party at Charlie Panucci's bus stop one block over on Henry Street. Tomorrow I'd be out there with her.

Chapter 2

*E*ric's daydream is like a song he has stuck in his head. It doesn't make any sense, and he wishes it would go away, but there it is, hanging around.

Instead of a crusty sock sticking out of his cast, he has skis on his feet. Instead of spring mud, there's snow. And Janine, in her yellow ski jacket and her brother's boots, has her feet stuck deep in the snow. Her cheeks are pink, and her brown hair blows in the bright wind. "I'm coming!" he calls to her. "Don't worry!"

With one swooshing turn, like James Bond at the beginning of The Spy Who Loved Me, *he reaches her and with one arm pulls her out of the deep snow.*

In reality they'd both probably wind up head down in a snowdrift. In reality she's too strong and tough ever to get stuck in a mere snowbank. No, the only thing true about this dream is that Janine is in real trouble and that he, Eric, is the only one who can help her.

That's what he tells himself, anyway. It's nice to dream.

◎ *Janine*

My mother sat hunched over her business accounts, planning menus, running her fingers through her silvery hair, while I packed my own lunch. Plain peanut butter on good white bread, an apple, one of the chocolate puddings I made last night in little plastic containers. I prefer simple food. On the grocery list I wrote "Scooter Pies." Daddy already had made a note there: "Nature's Own Organic Granola—no raisins." Disgusting. Just because he was getting tubby, why should the rest of us suffer? Julia would soon have everyone in the family brainwashed, but not me.

A third child never gets consulted about anything. When Julia was in eighth grade, Mom was still home every day, cooking her catering foods in our kitchen. Now she was gone, with business in full swing. Naturally I was independent and self-sufficient because of it. There wasn't much choice. People who are the oldest child or the only child get asked: What kind of cereal do you want? Do you need a ride? Whom do you want to carpool with? Do you want to take Spanish or French?

Not in my family, where it was grab-what-you-can-get out of the cereal cupboard, where it was take-French/soccer/dancing school, Jeff-and-Julia-did, where car pools were formed with the first live volunteers. It didn't bother me.

For breakfast I ate Lucky Charms, and since no one was watching, I used the whole milk that was supposed to be saved for coffee. Julia gave me a cup of almond tea. I didn't touch it until she disappeared to floss her perfect teeth. After I tasted it, I drank it all. Tea usually tasted the way my mouth did when I'd been crying. This tasted like the Jerusalem orange blossoms that grew in June in the wetlands at the end of our street and filled up the whole neighborhood with their beautiful smell.

When I made my way to the bus stop in Jeff's ugly boots, there was Eric Gooch, balancing on the ice on his crutches. He was a shrimp with lanky, straight pale brown hair and eyes that lurked greenish and muddy under thick glasses. A complete dweeb. From what I'd seen of him in school, where he obviously thought he was smarter than all of us, it was not surprising that he broke his leg. Probably tripped over his famous telescope or fell off the roof after checking his so-called weather station. Of course this hadn't stopped me from plotting to sign his cast one way or other the very first day of term. I loved to sign casts even if I didn't know the person inside.

He must have had the impression that I liked him just because I'd signed his slimy cast. I didn't, and I didn't want to hear his chitter-chatter.

"Great weather for skiing, huh?" Sure, if you were a rich kid who could go.

"Nice having the bus stop in front of your house, huh?" Right, until some dweeb with a broken leg came along to wreck it.

"How are you doing on that notebook for Whole Learning?" As if I'd tell him!

One more thing: I didn't plan to lug his stuff for him. He could get his new bud-a-roony Charlie Panucci to haul his garbage.

ERIC

ERIC

SCIENCE OBSERVATION
FEBRUARY 8

Mr. Lincoln: This observation is based on a direct interaction with the subject. Pity me.

"You can't stand at this bus stop," said Janine. Speaking objectively, I'd say she has eyes the color of root beer, medium brownish red, and glowing flatly. She's short, compact, and neat and always stands perfectly straight. She could be cute if she didn't have such an attitude problem.

At first I stood there and said nothing. I adjusted my crutches and waited for the bus. One thing I've learned from studying meteorology is that if you're patient, something develops.

Janine glared at me, her red mittens on her hips, her perfectly broken-in hiking boots planted apart in the snow. "This is my bus stop," she said.

I dropped my backpack on the snowy ground in response. "Legally?" I asked. Janine turned her back to me, her arms in her down jacket crossed over her chest, doing the bus-waiting pose. She was still trying to persuade me to hobble over to Charlie's stop, though.

"The fact is," she said loudly, as if she were addressing all of Kingfisher Lane, "you think you're smart, but you're nothing but a dweeb. I don't associate with dweebs. This stop is for popular people. So it's not going to do you any good standing here."

"If you're so popular, why are you standing here alone?"

"My friends don't ride bus twenty-one. They ride bus thirteen. They live in another neighborhood." I wished she did, too. It was plain that she didn't think Charlie Panucci was popularity material, or Marcy Moreno, either. And she'd already told me what she thought of me.

"The fact is," I said calmly, "it's too far to the next stop. It's also a fact that you don't know the first thing about me. You don't know whether I'm a dweeb or anything else at all."

Janine wasn't really wrong. I am not what anyone would call cool. But skiing was cool, all right. It was the first truly cool thing I'd ever done, sliding through snow far prettier than the plowed-over mess back home, riding the chairlift when there was a windchill factor of -10° Celsius, watching the back of Dad's head as he led me down harder and harder slopes.

I tried for a little human sympathy. "I broke my femur, my thighbone," I told Janine's back.

She turned quickly to look. She couldn't help herself. "How nauseating," she said. Pretty nasty.

The bus came steaming up and opened its door. Janine stamped up the steps, ignoring me as I balanced on one crutch to reach for my backpack.

"*Hey!* What's the matter with *you?*" The bus driver's voice boomed into the street. I lifted my head to tell him about my skiing accident. He had a beard and a big belly and the name Barry stitched onto his jacket. Then I saw that he was addressing Janine. "Hop back down there and help your buddy with his book bag!"

Her buddy! She didn't like that. She bumped against me on purpose as she bent down. My backpack whipped past my face as she mounted the steps and disappeared down the aisle of the bus.

I heaved myself up the narrow steps and dropped into a seat. I waited. And waited. Finally, suddenly, my backpack whizzed into my lap.

"You'll be sorry!" Janine hissed into my ear.

Mr. Lincoln, you were right. Observing Janine will be a very interesting project if I survive it.

⊚ Janine

It wasn't like there hadn't been snow other years to get in the way of kickball. But the Kickball Club had never been daunted before. Last year after a big blizzard we even got out there with snow shovels and cleared enough infield space to play. Things were pretty hilarious in the outfield, what with Clark Jamison and Mike Marx diving for the ball and getting buried in snow, but it just made it more fun.

This year I brought my shovel, and everyone just looked at me.

"I don't have the energy for shoveling," said Kelly, the snot.

Susan gave me a sympathetic look and said, "We've only got ten minutes, anyway, Janine. Maybe by tomorrow it'll be melted."

"Fat chance," I said, and tossed the ball to Barbara, hard. She caught it in her stomach and gave me a questioning smile.

But before either of us could say a word, Artie O'Halloran zoomed up to her and snatched the ball away. "Keep-away!" he yelled.

I was after him so fast I didn't realize that Barbara wasn't with me. She was standing there neat and pretty by the wall, with neat and pretty Susan and Kelly, while I was sweating and panting and wet with snow. Well, who cared? I chased Artie up and down the banks of snow, filling my loafers with it. Just when I was at his heels, he threw the ball to John Heinz. John threw it back, and I intercepted it and took off at full speed.

The bell rang when I was as far from the doors as I could be, so I was last in line. I was standing there on one foot, the ball under my arm, panting, dumping the snow out of one loafer, when Kelly said, "Gosh, Janine, you sure do like to chase the boys."

I looked up at her and said, "You should know, Kelly." But it was Marcy Moreno, that new girl, who caught my eye. Even though she had her back to me, I could see her smile. She was laughing actually. At me? With me, I decided. For a second I almost laughed back. She had that kind of smile. But then she asked me to play soccer. Just me and her?

"It's not the right kind of ball," was all I said. I could hardly go play with Marcy after my so-called real friends had taken off. Then I stopped, because I remembered something Barbara had told me. "Is it true you have baby guinea pigs at your house?"

Her brown eyes shone. "Sixteen of them," she said. Cute, I thought. I bet they all slept together in a big ball. I would have liked to see them.

Ahead of us in line Kelly said something to Susan and Barbara, who burst out laughing. I might as well have not existed.

"Sixteen guinea piglets?" I said loudly. "I bet they stink!"

E R I C

SCIENCE OBSERVATION
FEBRUARY 13

Choose a quote from the list on the board and comment on it, keeping your subject in mind.
    "No man is an island."

Janine is standing outside in her driveway, looking up at the sky, her hands in her pockets. She wears a navy pea jacket that could have been her brother's first. It doesn't look new. Maybe she got it at one of those antique clothing stores Mom and I wanted to shop at last Thanksgiving in New York, but Dad wouldn't go in. Janine's cheeks get pink all the way down to her chin. Her father drives in, in his red pickup truck, and she stands there and waits for him. But when he gives her a kiss on the hair, she pulls away. He just laughs, though, acts like he doesn't care.

It's 16° on the Fahrenheit scale today, 7.5° Celsius. Winds out of the northwest gusting up to 30 knots. It doesn't look like a good week for kickball.

According to my observations, any weather is good weather for keep-away. I brought my video camera out at recess yesterday. I have to stay on the patio by the cafeteria, where the snow is shoveled.

It was boys against girls: Jerry Sutter, Artie O'Halloran, and Clark Jamison against Janine and Marcy and Cynthia Dankowitz. The cheerleader girls refused to take part. They sat on the wall and shivered and talked about people. That's what it looked like, anyway. Janine mostly tried to throw the ball to Artie, and Clark tried to throw the ball to Janine. Marcy tried to get Janine to throw her the ball, but Janine wouldn't, not once, until the end of the game. Then she yelled, "Hey, guinea! Hey, pig!" at Marcy. And when Marcy turned, she threw her the ball before Marcy was expecting it. Marcy caught it, though, and called back, "They are so *cute!*"

Cynthia Dankowitz went over to Marcy and asked, "What's cute?" Marcy answered in a voice too low to hear. Cynthia smiled and wiggled her fingers, something like the motion a guinea pig's feet would make. They walked into school together, and Janine went to find Barbara.

Interpretation? It boggles the mind.

✑ *Janine*

Ever since Mother started working, I'd hated to be alone in the house. A dog or a cat, any kind of pet, would have made a difference, but as it was, there was no warm spot in the house, no balls of fur in the chairs as there were at Barbara Finney's, no crazy dogs like Susan's. On days when Jeff and Julia weren't home, I walked down the street to the wetlands, part of the marshes that Marsh Park is named after. There was a pond there that belonged to me.

The pond acted like a mirror most gray afternoons, but today I was surprised to find it white, frozen and covered in snow. I hadn't been there since vacation, when we had that big snowfall that still covered the neighborhood. It surprised me. So did the dirt and boardwalk path, which was snow and ice now. Someone had been there, trudging along in boots bigger than Jeff's. I placed my feet in those footprints and made my way through the woods and swamps to the pond, my eyes intent on the path.

The pond was useful once. A stream poured into one end, and a river emerged from the other. Where the stream entered, trees and rocks stood watch against the sandy bluffs. Where the river flowed out, an old red mill sat, empty and waiting to rot, smelling faintly of apples from all the cider it had made.

It was a good thing the area was designated wetlands by the state. Otherwise the woods would have been mowed down and the swampy places filled up to make room for more houses. Even Daddy, who always needed good places to build, was happy that hadn't happened. He'd grown up skating on the pond during those wonderful years when it froze right through (it looked kind of mushy at the moment), and he'd have hated to see anything change it.

Now it belonged to me, to me and a fisherman I'd been seeing from a distance since around Christmastime. He wasn't out there now, but he had been there. I could see the trail he'd made when the ice was harder, out to a hole he could fish through. I guessed it was his footprints that I was walking in. I wished the pond, and the footprints, belonged to Artie and me and that the mill was our house.

I'd found a perfect valentine for Artie. It was a Peanuts card with Peppermint Patty and Charlie Brown on the baseball field. It said, "What a catch you'd be, Valentine." It was big and had a purple envelope. I wondered what Artie was cooking up for me?

E R I C

SCIENCE OBSERVATION
FEBRUARY 17

Janine lives in a yellow house across the street from me, and her bedroom is the left window on the second floor. I found that out one cloudy afternoon when the lights were on in that bedroom. I was on the roof checking the wind, and a movement in that window caught my eye. I've looked at the Gagnons' house from Katie's windows, which are at the front of our house, and noticed that you can't see in. But the roof was a different story. I saw Janine run into her bedroom and slam the door. She held on to the doorknob and leaned hard on the door, as though she were trying to keep someone out. Then she jumped and looked at the floor.

For a moment she disappeared from view, and then I dropped to the floor of the roof because she was coming right toward her window as if she'd seen me. I crouched behind the railing and adjusted the telephoto lens on my video camera, hoping the telescope helped hide me, but Janine didn't look up. Instead, she opened the window, pushed up the outside storm window, and dropped something into the bushes in front of the house.

Mysterious behavior! At last, something interesting to observe about Janine Gagnon.

But then all was revealed. Janine walked to her door and opened it, and her brother, Jeff, came charging in, a hockey stick in his hand. I took the opportunity to drag my leg over to the roof door and slip down the stairs, laughing. From behind the curtain in Katie's bedroom, I saw Jeff pawing through the bushes with his hockey stick. If I were more able bodied, I thought, I'd go help him. I thought the better of it when Jeff found his puck at last, dug it out of the snow, and started to go back into the house. The door was locked, and he was left standing on the steps, yelling, *"Janine!"* like Fred Flintstone yelling, *"Wilma!"* at the end of the cartoon.

Julia, their beautiful older sister, opened the door calmly and let Jeff in.

◗ *Eric*

I stopped watching the Gagnons when Katie came into her room and asked, "What are you doing, Ee-rack?"

I picked up my crutches and made my way down the hall to my room. Katie followed me. Her white cat, Mini Pearl, was sleeping on my bed.

"What did you call me?" I turned and looked at her like the kid from Mars that she is.

"Ee-rack," she said. "It's your name."

"No, it's not," I said. "What do you want, anyway?"

"I want to know what you were doing."

"Nothing," I said. "What did it look like?"

"Spying," Katie said.

"You know who's a spy?" I asked. "This cat. What's he always doing on my bed?"

"She," said Katie. "She always sleeps there. She thinks it's her bed."

"What am I supposed to do about it?"

"Pet her," Katie said. "You're lucky she wants to sleep on your bed. I wish she'd sleep on mine."

"It can be arranged," I said. I dumped the cat on the floor and lay down on my bed. It was warm where Mini Pearl had been.

Katie stood next to me. "Is it going to snow?" she asked, as if I were Meteorology Central.

I looked at Katie's face. She looks like me and Mom, but shorter, and pretty, with brown braids and such big green eyes. She wanted it to snow, that's what I thought.

"Yes," I said.

"How do you know?" she asked.

It was just too much information to go into right then. "I just know," I said. The fact was, it *felt* as if there would be more snow.

And there was.

☉ *Janine*

I thought I would go insane if the snow didn't end soon. One night I dreamed that I was skiing in my pajamas. I was cold, but the mountain was so beautiful. I don't know which mountain it was, Butternut or Mohawk or Southington, but I must have been high up on it, because it took forever to get to the bottom. And I was cold in those pajamas. Every time I thought I saw the lodge at the bottom of the mountain, a hill appeared between me and it.

But my skiing was beautiful, and the sounds my skis made were soft and hushed and clean.

At breakfast I told Daddy about my dream, leaving out the pajama part, and asked again if we couldn't go skiing just one time before the end of the season. He looked at Mother, and they both just frowned.

"It's not just the money, Janny," he said, and my mind

started to shut down. "I've got to get these bids in on the season's work, or we'll have another summer like last year."

"It's almost March," I said.

He sighed patiently. "Janny Pan. You know how this business works. Sometimes it's less fun than a barrel of—"

"Goldfish," said Jeff. I looked at him, and he raised one eyebrow at me, trying to be sympathetic, but I wasn't in the mood.

I stood up and pulled my ski jacket on. "Look," I said, flipping over my lift tickets. "We haven't been a single time this year. And we're not going, are we? Not this weekend or any other, right?" I was yelling, trying to keep the tears back.

I didn't even know why I was so upset until after lunch that day when everybody was standing around shivering in the playground. I was standing there with the kickball, hoping somebody would play, and Clark Jamison came and yanked it out of my hands. And Marcy Moreno, of all people, took off after him before I even made a move. Well, a few of us had played keep-away once before. It wasn't my idea of a great game. But suddenly the whole class got involved, all but that Gooch kid with the crutches.

Charlie Panucci went after Marcy, who tossed it to Barbara, who dodged Artie and threw the ball to Kelly. Kelly ran, bouncing every which way, with everyone's eyes on her, and I couldn't help laughing. John Heinz went after her, and she fell into the snow, the ball rolling away. I scooped it up, and the game went on, but just then it seemed like there was something more going on than keep-away. Whenever Barbara had the ball, Artie went after her. If I had it, it seemed like dweebish little Clark always came after me.

Well, at least we all were playing something. Still, I was glad when the bell rang and we lined up. I couldn't look at anybody, just stared in the direction of people's waists, and that's when I noticed Barbara and Susan and Kelly. They all were wearing their ski jackets, like me, but instead of last year's tags they had tags from last weekend. February 22, it said, on yellow tags from Butternut. Last Saturday. They'd gone skiing together. And they hadn't asked me.

Chapter 3

*I*t's all Janine's fault that this is happening. She promised not to come, yet here she is again. Stupid. Dweebish. All her fault. She feels helpless, standing here, a victim, the way she used to feel around the other girls when she was small. Second grade was the year when they'd started to group off into twos and threes. "I'll be your best friend," they'd wheedle and whine. Her best friend? Sure, if only she'd play their way, share her cookie, let them go first. And if she didn't? They'd turn their backs on her, make significant little faces at each other, and walk away with that snotty swing to their shoulders.

What else could Janine do, back then, but strike first? Knock their drawings from the desk and walk on them, leaving footprints, so that they'd cry out as though pinched. Bump into them in the cafeteria when they were drinking so that they'd choke and spit their milk. Worst of all, sit with another girl and whisper, and look at them.

By sixth grade they were solid: Barbara and Janine and Susan and Kelly, like the Four Musketeers, playing kickball and singing in the parish show, sleeping over at one another's houses and staying up all night talking, like as not about *the dweebs in the class. It was so much more comfortable to be inside a group than out of it, accepted, not a reject like those other girls.*

Here she is now, threatened again by someone who wants to make her feel—what? Bad? Embarrassed? Turned on? Certainly not turned on; she shudders at the very words.

Janine curls her toes in the sand and feels her fists turn into stones. She'd like to stomp the part of him that scares her so. What else can she do now but strike first?

E R I C

SCIENCE OBSERVATION
FEBRUARY 26

You asked us to describe a defining moment for the subject of our observations, Mr. Lincoln, and here it is. It didn't take long to observe one, considering the subject is Janine.

When Coach Dillon asked if anyone had suggestions for what to do in gym in the month of March, Janine raised her hand and suggested dancing. She got shouted down by people who wanted floor hockey, but not before she got a chance to say that we'd all benefit from a head start on the tango.

For the first time in my life I didn't care what we did in gym, so I didn't vote. I could just sit back and relax and wonder whether they'd go for the ball game without thinking about what I would do if the ball came to me.

I did notice that when it came to a vote, most of the girls voted with Janine. I was sure the tango didn't mean that much to them, but nobody else seemed surprised. "They know what she'll say to them afterward if they don't vote with her," Charlie Panucci told me.

Marcy didn't follow the crowd; she voted for floor hockey. And when Cynthia Dankowitz saw Marcy sitting there with her hand up all alone, she raised hers, too. "I change my vote," she said casually. From the look Janine gave her, I'd say that took some courage.

⊚ *Janine*

There was something about all that snow on the ground that made the whole neighborhood echo with noise. Whenever the Gooch shut up talking about how the storms we had over the weekend weren't predicted by the *Farmer's Almanac* (shows what farmers know), I could hear the kids' voices all the way from Charlie Panucci's house. You could even hear Mousy Moreno. It sounded as if the snowball fight of all time took place out there every morning. They even let the little kids play.

So big deal for Mousy Marcy. I got her back good for not voting with me. I called her number and said I was Cynthia

Dankowitz. I asked her to come over to my house today and told her to bring her snow pants in a bag.

After school there was Marcy, digging her snow pants out of her locker and walking over to Cynthia. The looks on both their faces nearly killed me. I turned and raced as if I were seriously late for my bus. I held it in all the way home, even through watching Marcy climb onto our bus after all, looking as if she'd just gotten a pie in the face.

Finally I made it to my room, flopped on my bed, and laughed. Let her be friends with Cynthia if she wanted to. What would Cynthia think of sixteen baby guinea pigs—and two big parents? I could just see the look on her prissy face.

JANINE

SCIENCE OBSERVATION
FEBRUARY 28

Mr. Lincoln, I'm still working on finding a defining moment.

SCIENCE OBSERVATION
FEBRUARY 28

From the weather station I observed Janine's actions after
school today, through my binoculars and the zoom lens of
the video camera. She walked along the street, looking
grumpier than usual, in her jeans and those great boots. She
had her hands in the pockets of a ski jacket I haven't seen
before and was shaking one pocket with her hand, making
her last year's ski lift tickets jingle. I liked the peacoat better.

It's easy to get her on video, but it makes for boring
viewing. She makes it easy by trudging along looking
straight ahead, with not a glance toward my rooftop
weather station.

I have been observing Janine for a month now, and I
have learned two things:

1. If you don't give her a valentine, she stomps your
lunch. At least that's what Artie says.

2. She has an evil need to say rude things to that girl
who lives on Charlie's street, Marcy Moreno. Marcy was
in tears today over something Janine had said or done.
She was out in the hall with you, Mr. Lincoln, and I
overheard you say Janine's name. I record it here merely
as a matter of observation.

I wonder what Janine does in the wetlands, those mushy
meadows and closed-in woods that surround the pond at

the end of the street. That's where she disappeared from view today, and she was gone for an hour. She must be coldblooded (like a snake, how unsurprising).

⊘ *J a n i n e*

On the first day of March we had another giant snowstorm, the fifth blizzard this winter. We had March 2 off from school because of it, and the sun came out and everything was melting. That's the day Mother and Julia chose to gang up on me.

It started when Julia lost her temper and snapped at me to quit complaining about wearing Jeff's boots. (Last year, when my own nice green duck-feet boots from L. L. Bean still fit, it hardly snowed here at all.) Mother said placidly that my life was easy. I said my life was boring. Julia stamped her foot and made one of her typical statements: "Only the boring are bored."

Something about Julia: She was very rarely critical. No matter how many comments I made about her stick-out teeth and her too-wide rear and her wacko eating habits, she was usually pretty nice to me. So when she let me know she thought I was wrong, I felt, well, *really* wrong. Like it or not, I usually listened to Julia, even when she sided with Mother and Daddy. But not this time.

I told Mother I would do extra chores for a week if I could just have new boots. She lined up the corners of the invoices on her French desk and said, "Hardly. We have shoes and dresses to buy for dancing school." Gulp of fear. Then Julia got even more neurotic (something had been eating her lately), saying she didn't see how she was going to go to college without zillions of dollars in loans, and what kind of way was that to start life?

That's when I burst into tears. I said that Barbara Finney had furry Eskimo boots that she bought at a rummage sale. "Oh?" said Julia. "Miss Janine wants to shop at rummage sales?"

"It wouldn't hurt either of you," my mother said mildly, "and it would help your daddy and me." She made a note on her shopping list for the Chamber of Commerce St. Patrick's Day corned beef supper. As if *she* would ever wear second-hand goods.

"No!" I sobbed. "I just want pretty boots!" Even I realized that I sounded ridiculous. After all, the official start of spring was just three weeks away. I wouldn't need boots much after that, unless the weather continued its weird act.

I went to my room to catch up on my observations. I had begun to feel queer about observing myself. I didn't understand myself at all. The usual Janine would have made sure everyone's life was miserable during floor hockey since the girls had let dancing get voted down. But once I'd pulled that great trick on Marcy, the energy had gone out of the situation.

The fact was that I liked floor hockey, I liked going head to head with everyone in the class, especially now that spring was coming and there was the possibility of getting up baseball teams at recess. Even though the snow had melted off the playground, nobody played kickball at all, and keep-away had turned into one big chase. They didn't even bother with the ball, just ran until they caught someone (always someone of the opposite sex), then grabbed on and wrestled, pretending they wanted to get away from each other. Clark Jamison had tried it once on me, only once, before I pummeled him to the ground and left him there.

Mr. Lincoln said you should use your subject's actions to

figure out his (her) character, but what did I learn from pummeling Clark: that I hated his little guts?

After a while I gave up writing and went to the bathroom, and while I was in there, I heard them talking about me in Julia's room. "She hasn't had a friend over in the longest while," Julia told my mother. I stuffed my fingers in my mouth to keep from shouting out loud, "It's not my fault they're all dweebs and cheerleaders and nobody wants to just play kickball anymore!" I didn't say it. But Julia already knew. "They're all trying to grow up so fast, Mother. You know, Janny's mature in many ways, but she's a little behind the times that way." The sneak! So I was a little flat chested, and I didn't hang around the smoky school bathroom, curling my eyelashes and glomming on lip gloss. Did that mean I didn't have friends?

Mother's voice dropped so low I had to open the bathroom door a crack just in time to hear her say, ". . . so I told Monica Gooch we could carpool together since she can only fit one more into that little car of hers. I don't know why she's bothering with dancing school at all, to tell you the truth." Tears, actual tears, came to my eyes at the thought of carpooling with that weird little Eric Gooch. I started to feel that if I didn't get out of the house, I'd explode.

"Well, I don't know, Mother, but it's a good idea to throw her in with some new kids. Maybe she could use a new friend. I've seen her talking to Eric Gooch at the bus stop."

I slammed the door on the answer. I pulled on those boots and banged down the stairs as loud as I could. Was Eric Gooch my terrible fate for this spring term? All you had to do was look into those pale pea green eyes of his and listen to his droning voice to see that his head was completely empty. He was just as boring as I was. Sure, he'd be an ideal friend for Janny! What was going on in Julia's head, anyway?

I went to the wetlands and threw rocks into the pond, hard

as fastballs. The fisherman was across the pond, and he gave me a wave, but I stared back like a zombie. There are times when it feels good not to wave back.

◗ *Eric*

During the first week of March, my mother thoroughly lost her mind. As if she hadn't been working hard enough at her job as a temporary secretary all day, now she'd signed up for two crash courses in personal finance and real estate, at night.

"Thank God your dance class is already paid for," she said.

"What does it matter?" I asked. I was doing something I never could have done at Haycock. Katie and I were doing our homework at the kitchen table while Mom cooked hamburgers. Mini Pearl was curled in Katie's lap while she wrote out her spelling words (Katie, not the cat).

"You sure can't dance with that cast on your leg, Ee-rack," Katie declared. She had definitely decided always to say my name that way. I made fish lips at her, which was what I had decided to do when she said my name that way. Then I snapped out of it to agree with her statement.

"That's right," I said brightly. At the beginning of the term I had thought I would get sick of Katie when I was home all the time. So far that hadn't happened. I liked her Barbies, who had personalities Mattel had never planned on, and her habit of wearing her underwear on her head when she brushed her teeth, and the songs she learned in first grade and was always singing to herself. Best of all, she shared her ant farm with me. She said they didn't care that I was practically a stranger to them. She acted out conversations between the ants and gave them all names and personalities.

"You're going," Mom said, just as brightly.

"There's no reason to go," I said practically. "I won't be able to dance." It was one thing to be sidelined in gym. But to sign up for an activity I couldn't even try to do?

"Oh, you can learn a lot by just observing," Mom said. Had she been talking to Mr. Lincoln or something?

"The hamburgers are smoking a little," Katie commented. Mom turned them down.

"Observe the burned hamburgers," I said.

"Not burned yet!" Sometimes I felt that I didn't know my mom at all. What I mostly remembered about the years when I was just a day student at Haycock was comfort: warm pajamas and stories and butterscotch pudding and bed. Mom came with the house. She was always there, in jeans and a T-shirt, and always glad to hear my voice every night. She'd ask me questions: How was I feeling? Whom had I sat with at lunch? Did I like the new art teacher? When I was at school, Mom missed me.

Well, all that had changed. Mom was a different person entirely now that Dad was gone and I was home: She wore high heels and a suit to work and drove around in the car a lot, very busy. She was short like me, and her eyes were a much nicer green than mine, but her hair was just as flat. When she cooked, her hair kept falling out of the knot on the back of her head and hanging over the hamburgers.

"Oh!" she said, and flipped a burger with a solid slap. "Forgot to tell you! We're going to carpool with the neighbors."

Great. At least I'd get to ride with Charlie.

She went on. "What's she like, this Janine Gagnon?"

"Janine Gag-me!" I sputtered. "I already spend too much time with that little—"

"What? Five minutes at the bus stop?"

"It's the longest five minutes of my day," I told Mom. I didn't mention how much worse it had been getting, hearing Janine snicker behind me as she "helped" me up the walk at the end of the day, under orders from Barry, the bus driver. At least at school it was Charlie who helped me heave my carcass in and out of the building, of his own volition, not because Barry made him.

My mother put her hands on her hips and stared me down, but I couldn't tell her.

"Maybe you should get your hair cut, sleek and short," I suggested to Mom. Katie put the eraser end of her pencil to her lips and considered how it would look.

"I understand the kids in this neighborhood have had a little problem with Janine," Mom said. "How are you faring?"

"What kids? What problem? Who have you been talking to?"

Mom tapped her fingers irritably on the counter and looked at me sideways, eyebrows raised.

"Janine's the one with the problem," I said.

Mom shook her head and picked up the phone, dialing to find someone to park Katie with on nights we had finance/real estate and dancing school. Something told me I would find finance more enlightening than dance. Maybe we should switch.

☺ Janine

Cynthia Dankowitz crashed into me deliberately in the lunch line and made me knock a box of straws all over the floor. I picked up about ten and then figured no one was watching me, so I walked away and left the mess there. But Mr. "Honest Abe" Lincoln crooked his finger at me and made me go back and clean up the straws. "Isn't that what they pay the cafeteria ladies for?" I said.

But he just pointed that finger and said, "I hope this isn't going to be your defining moment, Janine." That made me stand still in shock for a minute. I'd been concentrating so hard on observing myself that it had never occurred to me to wonder if someone else might be observing me, too. I would have to watch everyone's eyes.

By the time I got to the cafeteria, just behind Cynthia and in time to step on one of her heels, there was only a little room left at my usual table. Cynthia walked by, dragging her shoe, and went to sit with Mousy Moreno. Kelly and Barbara saw me, smiled their shaky smiles, and moved apart to make room for my chair. I wasn't about to sit with Mousy! I ate quickly so I could get outside, get some air.

Susan was already out there, leaning on the wall and talking to John Heinz. That's when Clark Jamison ran by and knocked the kickball out of my arms into the bushes and ran away as if he wanted me to catch him. I went after the ball instead. I went to pull it out, and while I was in the bushes, I heard Barbara's voice.

"I can't ask *her*. My mom says there's only room in the car for two friends. And she lives all the way over—"

I looked up, and she was turning away, walking toward the basketball hoops, with Susan at her side saying something in her soft voice that I didn't catch.

Who was *her*? Kelly? Well, no, it couldn't be because Kelly lived just around the corner from Barbara. They were on the same bus, the one that went around the university. It was Susan who lived pretty far away, in an old farmhouse up on the hill.

And Kingfisher Lane was a separate bus from Barbara and Kelly *and* Susan. Was it me they were leaving out? From what? Just about any car could fit five: four girls and a mother. Me and Barbara and Susan and Kelly. The way it was supposed to be. The way it used to be.

◗ *Eric*

The person Mom found for Katie turned out to be Julia Gagnon, Janine's older sister. How convenient, she was right across the road and could bring Janine along when she came. Jeff baby-sat, too, his mother had said, but he went to bed early because he was "in training" for hockey practice at four-thirty each morning, the lucky stiff. I bet soon Janine would have hand-me-down ice hockey skates if she didn't already.

"Julia has grown up quite lovely and intelligent." Mom went blabbing on. "What a shame we've never spent much time with these neighbors."

What a shame. My mother didn't seem to miss her old life at all. No more fund-raising and volunteering and giving Christmas tree lightings for the lowly public. Now she was one of the lowly public herself, a regular working jane, as she put it. I had to admit she seemed to like it, no matter how worn out she got.

After dinner I worked my way slowly up the stairs to the roof. Time to take a few readings. Nothing was doing weatherwise: clear skies and cold air, getting warmer. Maybe a thaw. Mud would be rough on crutches.

I looked over at Janine's house, but the curtains were drawn over the yellow windows. At Haycock at this time of day Pete Hotchkiss would be out in the hall with his lacrosse stick, winging socks at the doorknob of the phone booth at the end of the hall. It would be dinner soon, and I'd be finishing up homework or taking readings off my windowsill instruments. I loved my mother and Katie, but I missed the guys at Haycock, where everyone was stuck together away from home. It didn't matter if you were a weatherhead dweeb (what Janine called me), not the way it did here.

I had asked Mr. Lincoln today about giving a daily weather report, and *she* had heard and yelled out, "Weather report! Why don't we just look out the window?" If it weren't for Charlie Panucci being friendly, I'd have been the class nothing. As it was, it felt like a charade. When I got my cast off, the guys would find out how lousy I was at sports, how I didn't even own Rollerblades, the way all of them did. Skiing had been great while it lasted, but Mom would probably never let me back on skis.

I took a deep breath. If I could just tough it out at this school until summer and camp— Well, that's the way I was used to thinking. But that's when it dawned on me, that night on the roof. If Mom didn't get back with Dad, I wouldn't be going back to Haycock at all. Somehow I had to. I just had to.

JANINE

SCIENCE OBSERVATION
MARCH 8

Mr. Lincoln: I can't find a better defining moment than this one.

Mr. Weatherhead Gooch was right about the thaw.

After school he went right up on his perch, looking at the sky through his binoculars, looking like a foolish dweeb, when I passed by on my way to the wetlands.

There was a lot of snow melting and a rushing brook had burst through its icy crust in the meadow by the pond. I did something wonderful and insane, something Julia or Jeff or my mother or father or Eric Gooch or Marcy Moreno would never dream of doing. I took off Jeff's boots and threw them in the snow. I took off my socks, rolled up my jeans, and stepped into the water.

Suddenly the sky and the air and the water became sharp and clear, and I was in the center of it all. I could feel the smooth pebbles of the brook bottom rolling under my toes. The water was as cold as a thousand heavy ice cubes, very fast and thin and bright and gurgling.

Without thinking I reached into my pockets, pulled out my red mittens and put them on my hands. They felt good, so warm and dry, but the joke was on me, because what did I need mittens on my hands for when my feet were naked in that winter water?

I laughed at myself, right out loud, throwing my head back to the blue sky, and when I opened my eyes, I saw a man. He was a tall man, young, with shiny dark brown hair and gray eyes, wearing an army jacket and sweatpants and boots like Jeff's. He must have been walking down the path just as I had. He held a fishing pole in his hand, and that made me recognize him as the ice fisherman I saw before.

I just stood there, appalled at being found, and he watched me for a second, smiling. I just felt like it, so I did it: I smiled back. He walked on into the woods. I guess he was leaving because the ice was too mushy to fish.

When he was gone, I climbed out quickly and dried my numb feet on my socks, pulled on my boots, and walked home.

E R I C

SCIENCE OBSERVATION
MARCH 9

Janine went to the wetlands again yesterday. She looked the same as she always does, going: fierce. She saw me, but she didn't wave, so neither did I. Coming back, she usually looks calmer, but I'll admit I didn't observe her return. No great loss, I'm sure.

I didn't bother to video her. I'm getting tired of her as a subject.

Hey, Mr. Lincoln! Is anyone observing me?

Chapter 4

*O*nce there was a kid at Haycock who wouldn't follow the dress code. He was a day student, and his parents both worked, so if he came to school in jeans or a shirt without a collar, they couldn't come get him or bring him the right clothes. His game was to try to slip past the teachers. Red socks, a beaded belt, that kind of thing. He got suspended for wearing white sneakers outside gym class for a week solid. Pete Hotchkiss, who always knew the gossip, said the kid would just smack his head and act like he'd forgotten every single day, then make a big show of going to the office to call his mother, who he knew wasn't home. The dean sent out a letter saying that refusal to follow the rules was antisocial behavior and could be grounds for disciplinary action.

Eric still doesn't get it. What's antisocial about clothes? It seems like the worst thing you could do was go without clothes. Witness the way guys at school would go berserk when someone stole their bathrobes while they were in the shower and they had to run back to their room naked. Still, that's kid stuff. What really feels wrong is when an adult does it.

Eric thinks about what Janine said the man at the pond did. If there is anything that is antisocial, that is. And he *wishes it wasn't up to kids to do something about it. Most of all, he wishes it wasn't up to him.*

◗ *Eric*

Dad called. I answered.

"Dad! How did you get through?"

He cleared his throat. Inappropriate question, that sound said.

"How are you, Ric?" That name.

"Where are you?"

"I'm a mile high," he said. He had decided to be cheerful. "Denver." Well, I found out later that meant Denver was a mile above sea level, but at the time I didn't know what he was talking about.

"Oh," I said stupidly.

He wasn't calling to talk to Mom. He wasn't calling to tell us what he was doing or where he was (other than the name of the city) or whether he was coming back or wanting a divorce or sending me back to Haycock. He was calling about camp.

He had heard about this tremendous golf camp from "a colleague of mine, a lovely lady," and thought it would be just the thing this summer for recovering me. He was all business, all cheerful business. I sat there in the hallway at the foot of the stairs, holding the phone, trying hard to breathe. Naturally, after almost two months of being completely missing in action, he was stepping back into my life to tell me what my next step up the ladder of success should be?

I wanted to argue, to yell, to tell him what I thought about his driving away and leaving me in the emergency room. Instead, I heard myself telling him about something I'd heard John Heinz talking about at school. Some cousin of his had gone to a wilderness camp.

"If you're going to survive in the business world," said my father, "golf is a great game to get under your belt."

If ever there was a game that focused on a ball, it was golf.

"This wilderness camp is great, Dad," I said. "They teach you all about living in the woods," I said. "You learn astronomy and weather signs and what to eat and how to stay warm. It's cool."

"Ric, you already know plenty about weather. Golf is cool, too. I'd like you to give it a chance."

When my father said he'd like me to do something, that meant it had better happen. There wasn't usually much use in arguing, but something had gotten into me.

"Dad. I can't think of anything better to help me *survive* than survival camp."

"Is that what it's called?" His voice was sarcastic.

"No. It's Northeast Wilderness College."

"So you'll be majoring in berries and flint?"

What? He was suddenly much less than cheerful.

"Dad—"

"As long as I'm paying for it, I'd like it to be something I'm all for. And I'm all for golf camp."

"I'm going to ask Mom," I said. There was a silence on the phone.

"You're going to golf camp, Gooch," Dad said.

It was enough to make me want to break my other leg. I hung up the phone with a bang, and I didn't stop banging for a good ten minutes. I held my right crutch in my right hand and banged it against the wall all the way downstairs, hitting the wall with every step.

In the empty kitchen I stood looking out at the afternoon sunshine falling out of the trees into the backyard. I banged my crutch with all my might against the cabinet door under the sink.

"Eric?" Mom was at the kitchen door, with a grocery bag in each arm. Behind her Katie dawdled in the driveway, dropping pebbles in the puddles of melting ice.

"He wants me to go to golf camp!" I said darkly, and banged my crutch along with every word.

"*Golf* camp!" Mom was so astonished I had to smile. "Golf camp?" she asked again, as if she hadn't heard right.

"Golf camp," I said. The words had begun to sound as absurd as the name on a can of cat food. I might as well have been saying "Fancy Feast" for all the sense it made.

"Oh!" Mom exclaimed fake joyfully. "Golf camp!"

She was definitely losing her mind. Why hadn't *she* wondered where he'd gotten the new phone number? Why didn't she want to know what else he had said? And what was she going to *do* about golf camp?

Mom stood there laughing, and I gave up wondering why and laughed back. My mother was funny. My mother was a lunatic. Who knew?

A bag of groceries slid sideways on the counter and tipped over, dumping a plastic container of strawberry yogurt onto the floor. I reached out a crutch and smacked it the length of the floor, golf style. "Fore!" I yelled.

"Well, look at that." Mom grinned, tucking that crazy loose strand of hair around the frame of her glasses.

"Yes, I hardly need golf camp," I said. "My talent is obvious. Anyway, I'm not going there."

"No?" Mom raised an eyebrow in a way she must have worked on in the mirror.

"I heard about this wilderness camp at school," I said, but

Mom held up her hand. It was at that moment that I first noticed she wasn't wearing Dad's ring, her big diamond.

"I want you home this summer," she said. "Unless—"

She stopped.

"Unless what?"

Mom put her hands on my shoulders and leaned her forehead against mine. I was still pretty short for my age. Only Michael Marx and Clark Jamison were shorter out of the Whole Learning class. "Eric John Gooch the Third," she said, "don't you know how much I want you home?"

I hugged her back and thought about it. What kind of kid was I, who could just go live at Haycock for the last three years and never question it, not really ever be homesick? I'd always known I would go to Haycock, that's all. There hadn't ever been a choice; it was just something sure to happen. I was beginning to wonder if I'd ever be as sure of anything in my life, ever again.

JANINE

SCIENCE OBSERVATION
MARCH 15

Yesterday in floor hockey I hit the ball into Kelly Kim's leg and got accused of doing it on purpose. The fact was that I didn't, but so what if I had? She and Barbara and Susan are definitely carpooling to dancing school together. And Kelly had the nerve to tell me, then suggest that I drive with Marcy Moreno. But Marcy looked up coolly and said that she was driving with Charlie Panucci, thank you very much.

"Maybe Janine could, too?" Barbara joined in, as if she were running for class president.

"Charlie's mother can fit only one extra because she has to bring her other kids when she drives."

"Won't it be great?" said Kelly, changing the subject. "I'm so nervous!"

"Oh, me, too," said Marcy.

"You're just nervous because no one's going to ask you to dance," I pointed out to both of them.

"It's okay if they don't," Marcy said. "I'll just ask them."

Barbara laughed, and I said under my breath to her and Susan and Kelly, "She thinks she's so great."

"Don't say that, Janine," said Susan.

I decided to take matters into my own hands. I had had enough lonely weekends and boring afternoons. When the bus got to school this morning, I was down the aisle at top speed, leaving the Gooch to fend for himself. I could see Barbara and Kelly leaning on the wall, waiting for the first bell to ring, and I made my way right over to them.

They had their heads together, but I leaned right in and said, "Listen to this!"

"Oh, hi, Janine," said Kelly in a bored way. She was a lot to put up with lately. But Barbara gave me her usual big smile.

"Julia's taking me to Skateland tonight," I said. "She's meeting some boy, and she doesn't want to go alone."

"Roller-skating?" asked Kelly. "Isn't she a senior in high school?"

I gave her my worst frog face. "Everybody roller-skates," I said. "Don't you?"

Susan Hackman got out of her father's car and came dashing over.

"Susie!" yelped Barbara and Kelly with an enthusiasm they had not shown when I arrived. I really didn't care anymore what Kelly thought. But Barbara and I had been friends since nursery school, and I wasn't about to let Kelly edge me out.

"So what do you think, Barbara?" I asked. "Want to come?"

Barbara Finney looked at Kelly and Susan and said, "Who's coming?"

Susan said, "Where?" at the same moment that I told Barbara, "Just us, so far. Me and Julia and Jeff and you."

"Skateland," Kelly told Susan.

"Jeff's going?" asked Barbara. Her smile gave me the oddest feeling in my stomach. Wasn't it enough to come with just me?

"Anyone can go," I said, glancing at Kelly and Susan.

"Okay," said Barbara, still smiling.

The bell rang, and Kelly and Susan just stood up and walked away. Barbara whirled to go with them, but I'm not this fast on my feet for nothing.

"We can pick you up at six," I said.

"That's okay," Barbara said. "I'll get my mother to drop us off." So they would all be coming, I thought. It would be like it always was.

But it wasn't.

[Stapled shut]

MR. LINCOLN: DON'T READ THIS!! PRIVATE!

I have one question in my mind that I observe keeps going around and around no matter how much I try to get my brain to change the subject: Will Artie O'Halloran dance with me?

SCIENCE OBSERVATION
MARCH 21

What is fascinating about videoing a floor hockey game is that it moves so fast that you can't focus on people but only on small squares of action. Today I tried it for the first time. What would happen was I'd train my lens on someone and follow him or her all over the floor. Other people would move in or out of the square, and I'd have to decide whether or not to follow them. Eventually I'd followed the game from one end of the floor to the other, seeing it through different people's eyes along the way.

Take Marcy Moreno, for example. She was too tall to play floor hockey really well. It was more for the little, wiry types like Janine and Artie and Mike Marx and, yes, Susan Hackman (another surprise). Marcy was never in front, charging down the court. She never scored a goal. She never tackled anybody directly to challenge for the ball. What Marcy was good at was slipping into empty spaces and stopping the ball from advancing down the gym toward her goal. She stopped Charlie *a lot,* I noticed when I viewed it later.

Barbara Finney was another interesting study. Just to listen to her (with those great cheerleading lungs), you'd think she was the center of the action. Her role, as she saw it, was not to advance the play but to encourage everyone else. She just ran along, chestnut braids flopping, looking like she was about to do something any minute, but barely even moved her stick toward the ball. "Good try!" "Yee-ha!" "Go, Janine!"

Nobody else cheered for Janine. They were too busy watching out for her. It was hard to believe she had nominated ballroom dancing when the vote came up, seeing how good she was at hockey. Another puzzle.

I said as much to Artie O'Halloran when he turned his ankle and came limping over to sit beside me. "Yeah, she's good at everything like this," he said. "Too bad she can't move away somewhere to train for the Olympics."

"Is she that good?" I felt stupid the minute I said it.

He laughed, then winced as he pressed an ice bag against his ankle. "No, I guess not. I don't know. I'm not sure she really likes to play like you have to for the Olympics. She just wants to wipe everybody out."

"Why?" I turned the camera back on Janine, so Artie wouldn't see my face. I myself had never been any good at games like this. At Haycock everybody knew that. But here nobody knew much of anything about me yet. As far as they knew, I was the fastest thing on two legs—except that one of them was broken. That cast was my excuse to sit on the sidelines and watch. Still, Artie was the kind of guy who made me nervous. He didn't have any use for somebody who wasn't a player. He would never have sat here to keep me company if he'd known how I played. So I turned the camera back on and watched Janine through my lens in a way that I hoped seemed casual and businesslike.

It was as if Janine were all alone on the court when she was playing, dodging in and out after the ball. But I caught her face in the zoom lens when she scored a goal. Marcy came up and clapped her on the back. Mike Marx passed by, scowling. Barbara was yelling something like "JA-nine! JA-nine! JA-nine!" But Janine, of all things, turned shy. She seemed to know they only liked her for scoring. Her eyes were turned to the floor, and the tips of her ears went red.

"Who knows what she wants?" said Artie, sounding tired. "I don't care."

"Maybe she'll change," I said. "How do you know she doesn't want to change?"

"This is Janine Gagnon we're talking about," Artie said.

▶ *Eric*

It was the last Friday of March, and I'd stayed home from school for a doctor's visit. That afternoon Charlie came to the door on his Rollerblades, bringing me my homework as an excuse to get a look at the gym class video.

I was in Dad's leather La-Z-Boy chair with the remote control in my lap, going through weather tapes I'd been making all March. I was trying to see if the weather through the spring equinox was following any kind of pattern. When Charlie came in and saw what I was watching, I expected him to get alarmed: Uh-oh, dweeb alert!

I decided just to be businesslike about it. "Weather," I said.

"What about it?" he asked.

"That's what I'm watching," I said.

He watched for a moment with me. In the video the sun was rising over the Gagnons' house, into a sky like the scales on a mackerel.

He shrugged and said, "What does it mean?"

"Mackerel sky," I said. "Lots of quick changes."

"Well, that's life," said Charlie.

"That's weather," I said.

I gave him the gym tape to put on, and for a few minutes we watched in silence.

"I can't get used to being in gym with girls," I said at last. The screen was filled with Susan at the moment (not for the first time, either), and I just had to say something.

"Sure," he said, "and you're not even letting them see you in your shorts. Last year Clark forgot to wear his jock, and right in the middle of gymnastics—"

"Oh, no." I laughed. "Don't tell me."

"When he was on the parallel bars—" We were doubled over, laughing.

"Do you miss your old school?"

Talk about distraction. Charlie's question surprised me into being honest. "It was like home," I said.

Charlie shook his head. "I can't believe you lived away like that. My mother would have a cow."

"Mine didn't like it," I said. "But Dad did it when he was a kid. There wasn't any choice. Now that he's gone—"

"So it's not just a money thing?"

I didn't say anything. Charlie waved his hands in the air as if to wipe out what he'd just said.

"Only partly," I said. "Mostly it's Mom."

Charlie smiled. "How did you get around to school and all?"

"Well, all the buildings were pretty close together. We walked."

"Should have got Rollerblades," said Charlie. He had undone his and left them in the doorway and was sitting on the couch with his sock feet up on the coffee table.

Here the cool kids all had Rollerblades. Even the uncool kids did. At Haycock skates were kind of a street thing. There everybody talked about soccer shoes. You had to have the right kind, and everybody knew the price of the different models. I had a $125 pair of Adidas upstairs even now, rotting away while my feet grew out of them after only having

been in them about a month before my accident. There kids
had season tickets to the Knicks. Here they had basketball
hoops in the driveway. There kids had horses in their back-
yards. Here there was hockey in the street.

"It's all the girls." I excused myself. "I haven't known very
many, except in centerfolds of magazines."

Charlie stopped laughing and looked at me. Maybe he
didn't know what magazines.

"You know. We had them at school. Girls in . . . positions.
Girls with guys. Girls doing things with guys. Girls with girls
even." Any guy at Haycock would have joined in the discus-
sion with a scenario of his own. Charlie just looked astonished.

"Where'd you *get* them?" he asked.

I shrugged. "Everybody had those magazines. Sometimes
the dads even brought them or sent them."

Charlie shifted around in his seat. "The girls at school are
nothing like that, Gooch," he said.

"Oh, no? How about that Kelly—"

"It's different when you've known them since kindergarten. Even Kelly. She threw up once, in fifth grade, you
know?"

"What difference does that make?"

"When you've known them all your life, they don't really
thrill you." I didn't believe him, not about Kelly.

"It's my leg, too," I said. "The minute I'm off these crutches I'll move over to your bus stop." And something told me
I'd be campaigning pretty hard for Rollerblades.

He nodded. "Janine's got a problem," he said. That was
Panucci. He gave people a break. Still, he wasn't at Janine's
bus stop, so I had to wonder why.

Outside, Jeff Gagnon was in the street with his hockey
stick, trying to knock a little ball into a can laid on its side. If

we went outside, Charlie would play with Jeff. If we stayed in, he might think I was boring. "Let's go outside," I said.

So he put on his Rollerblades and skated around with Jeff. I used a crutch to try to hit the ball into the can, figuring that even if I did badly, they'd think it was just the crutches. I looked at the sky, which was clearing, and wondered where I would be this time next year: at Haycock or Marsh Park?

When Janine came stalking up the street from the wetlands, lugging an armful of cattails, Jeff and Charlie and I were all taking shots at the can. They each had a crutch, and I was walking around with the help of a couple of hockey sticks. She looked at us as though we were worms flooded out of the yards by the rain and elbowed her way to her gate, saying, "Pardon *me*."

J A N I N E

SCIENCE OBSERVATION
APRIL 2

Jeff is like Daddy, always trying to get everyone to lighten up, like life is supposed to be one big joke. Well, maybe it is to Jeff. I think if you're a boy, all you have to do is be good at sports. Being tall doesn't hurt, either, or good-looking. Jeff is all those, plus funny when he wants to be, so naturally everyone likes him. I mean, he was outside today with Charlie Panucci and Eric Gooch, of all people. Panucci is a good skater, so naturally he'd show up. But the cripple? What was *he* doing, hanging out with them?

Jeff never got involved in any of my school-bus arguments. He always said it was Julia's fault for starting the "littlest first" rule and for keeping it going even when I wasn't the littlest anymore. And if I was going to punch people out, he wasn't going to help me do it. "It's not like they're being mean to you," he said. Mother of course didn't get involved. She thought trouble between kids should be worked out between kids. That's why I still have hockey pucks shot under my door. And it's why nobody's at my bus stop anymore: They all went crying to *their* mothers, who did get involved.

It's not like Jeff has to rely on the neighborhood for friends. When the phone rings around here, most of the time it's for him. The rest of the time it's for Julia. Mother and Daddy got their own separate lines—for work—years ago. I can't remember the last time Barbara called, or even Susan or Kelly. It was obvious that none of them did anything anymore without seeing what the others thought first. If I could just get Barbara away from them . . . Well, I tried. I invited Barbara to go skating. And look what happened! Now she'll probably never speak to me again.

I wish I could get my mother involved now. I wish I could get her to call up Mrs. Finney and ask her why she didn't bring her daughter to Skateland Friday night like she was supposed to. If Mother did call, then Barbara would know I was lying. But I had to lie, and you'll see why.

Jeff's friends all showed up. Julia just happened to bump into the very guy she'd hoped would be there, a dweeb named Lionel. And it seemed like the whole rest of the rink was taken up with somebody's birthday party from downtown. It was a disgusting feeling, skating around by myself, feeling like everybody there must think I was trying to crash their party. I skated with Jeff for a little while, with him and his hockey friends, but then they went off to play pinball, and I was on my own. Then there was the couples dance, when they turned off all the lights except the blue ones and turned the mirror ball on. I went and leaned on the wall by myself, rolling my feet back and forth under me, and it felt like the end of everything good.

Monday morning I went leaping off the bus ahead of everyone. I ran over and grabbed Barbara. "April Fool!" I yelled. "You're an April Fool!"

She stood there and stared at me as though I'd gone insane, but I expected that. Susan and Kelly stared, too.

"Friday night, right?" I said.

"What about it?" She flipped a braid over her shoulder and looked nervous.

"Well, I didn't show up, did I?" I said. Susan and Kelly were watching me very seriously.

"Oh," said Barbara, perplexed.

"April Fool!" I said. "It was all a joke!"

Well, what else could I do, Mr. Lincoln? To borrow a sentence from Julia, I had my *dignity* to consider.

"That's a pretty stupid joke," said Susan, poking her pointed nose in.

"It didn't matter, anyway," said Kelly. "Barbara came to my house."

Barbara was forced to say, "I didn't go to Skateland, Janine."

Just as I'd planned, I acted. I pretended to laugh my head off.

"I'm glad to see you're not disappointed," said Barbara. "I tried to call, but the line was busy."

Well, how could it be, with Julia and Jeff and me all at Skateland? I held that thought because I could hardly voice it.

I'm writing this to let you know, Mr. Lincoln, that from here on in, I stand alone.

Chapter 5

*T*he grass on the bluff above the pond is long and soft, and Eric is tired from climbing. He lies flat out in the grass and adjusts his glasses, rests his worried eyes. Beside him, his little sister, Katie, slips a strip of grass between her fingers. She's trying to make it whistle.

Up above, the clouds have begun to regroup themselves. The sky seems something like the curtain at the front of a stage: What's going on behind? His weak leg is throbbing; the strong one is just plain tired from being depended on so much. At least, Eric tells himself, I know I'll be able to get up here when the time comes. When it happens, let it happen slowly.

Katie leans over and lets her braids tickle Eric's face. "I'm making you a mustache," she says, pulling one braid under his nose from the left and the other across from the right.

Eric lowers his brow dramatically and says in a growly voice, "You must pay the rent!"

Katie cups her hands around her ears, miming giant hair bows, and trills, "I can't pay the rent!"

"You must pay the rent!"

"I can't pay the rent!"

"You must!"

"I can't!"

He sits up, throwing off his "mustache," and holds an imaginary bow tie under his chin. "I'll pay the rent," he says in a proud, deep voice.

She knows the routine so well. She clasps her hands together at her cheek and coos, "My hero!"

But he hushes her, looking over her shoulder toward the edge of the bluff and the pond beyond.

He thinks back to the words written in a green notebook, words about a dark-haired man. He wonders what might happen if Janine met the man again. What does she think? What does she really think? Janine's not boy-crazy like the other girls, not as mature as the other girls, either, her sister, Julia, says. But, seriously, folks, how many mature people do you really know? He guesses he's more mature than lots of the adults in the neighborhood. None of them is looking out for Janine. None of them knows what he knows about her. None of them knows the danger she's in.

"What is it?" Katie says, almost too loud.

"Those clouds," he says, and lifts the camera from his lap to view the coming storm.

☺ *J a n i n e*

On Wednesday the PTA called to remind me that dancing school would start Friday night. Julia, who had dived on the phone when it rang, gave me the message. I got the jitters right away.

I asked Julia to teach me a little of the tango, but she said she hardly remembered it and I should ask Jeff. He didn't even look up from his geometry but just said easily, "There is no reason in this world for anyone to learn the tango. You will never have the need or opportunity to do it," in such a couldn't-care-less voice that Julia and I looked at each other and smiled in an evil way.

Julia grabbed me and put her cheek against mine and steered me across the kitchen floor. I tripped over my own feet, stomped on Julia's. She yelled, "Ouch!" nice and loud. We finished by bumping into Jeff's chair. "Oops!" said Julia, and waited.

Jeff got up. He was knocked out of his seat, actually. He stood there glaring. "You're doing it wrong," he said. He sat back down.

Julia gave me a knowing look. We kept going, with her stepping all over my feet and me trying to dodge her, until Jeff said, "Julia, are you supposed to be the man or the woman?"

She just laughed and said, "Who cares?"

"Pretzelhead!" Jeff called her. He got up and shoved her out of the way and put his arm around me, and danced with me. He smelled not of BO like usual when he comes close to me (which he does to make me smell his armpits after hockey, and the stinky insides of his skates, too) but like the cold still-winter air outside and his flannel shirt. His cheek against mine was a little scratchy, which was a surprise, because it didn't look it. Who only knows what my feet were doing? Jeff had me going up and down the kitchen and tipping over backward and spinning like I wouldn't have believed possible and giggling the whole time I did it.

After a few whirls he dropped me into the chair he'd been sitting in, grabbed his books, and headed for the stairs. "It's your night to start dinner, Julia," he said, as if to punish her for making him dance with me.

Julia shook out her long hair to rebraid it, and said to me, "See?" All I could do was nod my head, because I knew even more now that I couldn't wait to do the tango with Artie O'Halloran. But there was something else, too: Now I knew why all the girls were after Jeff. It wasn't just because he could dance.

E R I C

SCIENCE OBSERVATION
APRIL 6

Here you have it, Mr. L: defining moment #2.

The first night of dancing school Janine and Julia came over together, like Cinderella and the ugly stepsister. Guess which one I got to go out with? Julia curled up on the couch with Kate and *The Hobbit*, and I wanted to hang up my crutches and stay home. But I knew Mom would be along soon enough to haul me off to my doom, with Janine riding shotgun.

Then Janine caught my attention with a loud "Hey!" She was wearing a purple dress and sitting on the piano bench with Mini Pearl purring—traitorous cat!—on her lap. "Your cat's got a tick," she said in her toughest voice. She plied her fingers carefully through Mini's fur and slowly drew out the tick, without tweezers or matches or anything, just bare-handed. She was so gentle that Mini never even flinched.

The tick hung there, legs wiggling, its body looking half full of blood. With a flick of her fingertips, Janine squished it, then held it out to me. "Can I have a tissue or something?" she asked.

"Time to go," Mom said. I wondered if Janine planned to wash her hand before she started dancing.

As for Janine herself, I'll say one thing: She can dance. Yes, from the sidelines, where I was stuck, tapping my good left foot, I observed quite a bit about Janine. Namely, that she is not the only good dancer or, to judge by the looks on the faces of my "colleagues" (what the snooty, gorgeous teacher Miss Seal and her crabby, bossy mother, Mrs. Seal, call them), anyone's favorite. She'll never be what Bert, the very peculiar, green-jacketed teacher, calls a hot number. Still, she is one of the first chosen to dance every time, and why?

It certainly is not the look on her fierce face. It isn't her dancing talent, which the guys don't ever notice. They're having such trouble keeping their feet going in the right direction while having their arms around an actual human girl that they don't know if they're doing the waltz or the electric slide.

No, fellow scientist, this is what I observed: Janine gets a lot of partners because she is short.

✑ Janine

Mr. Lincoln stood boring and solemn beside his desk, looking like Fred Flintstone in cowboy boots. "If you were observing an owl in the forest, would you merely say"—and here his fingers became an owl's flapping wings—" 'The owl flies to the pine tree, the owl flies to the oak tree'? No, you would say, 'The owl flies from tree to tree, looking for a nice mouse dinner.' " We all sat at our desks with round, sleepy eyes, like owls I've noticed at the wetlands in the daytime.

"What I want you to add to your observations in the remaining weeks—and this is the middle of April, people, halfway through the term!—is interpretation, a little theorizing, about why you think your person behaves as he or she does. Do not merely observe."

Thanks to Mr. Lincoln, I was sitting at the kitchen table with Julia and her new boyfriend, pretending to look over my notebook. There was nothing in my observations that I could improve on, but there was plenty that I'd like to change about *this* situation.

His name was Lionel Carlton, and he was here in our kitchen for the second time in a week. They were drinking almond tea and laughing about some big story they were thinking of writing together about the drama club. Lionel had tan hair that waved back from his forehead, and a white V-neck sweater, and dark blue eyes behind square-rimmed glasses. He wore soft, worn-in brown hiking boots and green socks. I wasn't paying a bit of attention to what they were talking about, only to how Julia was acting, throwing her hair back from her face and grinning up at Lionel with a fleck of tea leaf on her teeth.

Jeff came home. He shook his head at me to get me to leave the kitchen, and with a shrug I took my books and slogged upstairs. Jeff stuck his head in my room and said, "Guess what role Lionel has in *The Wizard of Oz*?" That's the play the high school was putting on; Julia was working backstage.

"Toto?" I was so funny I made myself laugh sometimes.

"The scarecrow."

"Oh!" I hooted. "If he only had a brain!"

"But he's cute, isn't he?" Jeff wiggled his eyebrows at me; it's a talent we share. "I can tell you think so!"

"You're *such* a dweeb."

He cooed, "Ooh, Lionel!" in a voice that sounded nothing like Julia's. I stuck my foot out and slammed the door shut, just barely missing Jeff's head.

He just laughed. "Reflexes!" he bragged.

He should have let me stay in the kitchen. Why had I listened when Jeff asked me to come upstairs, anyway? I mean, what had Julia done for me lately?

I opened the door a crack. "Next time, you're dog meat," I said to Jeff. I banged the door closed before he could react.

He went into his room and turned his music on, *loud*.

J A N I N E

SCIENCE OBSERVATION

APRIL 16

Here I sit, me and my observation journal. What do you want, anyway, Mr. Lincoln? I'm sick of thinking about myself, writing about myself, observing myself. I feel trapped in this house. It would be great if Julia and Jeff would come into my room and play Monopoly, like we used to on rainy days. That was nice, even when I was sure they were cheating me just for the fun of it, because I was little and dumb. Everything was nicer when we were little kids. It's really not fair that some people always get to be older and others always have to be younger. I'm as old now as they were then, back in the Monopoly days. If they came and played with me now, I'd rip them, I'm sure of it!

It's raining now, and things inside look even darker and glummer. Mother's going to be out all afternoon, planning the Easter Bunny lunch she is catering for the Women's Club. Julia is cackling like a lunatic downstairs in the kitchen with that dweebish Lionel. Jeff's music doesn't quite muffle her noise, and it is thumping against my wall.

I observe about myself that I am getting a headache. I interpret the headache as a response to the environment of this house. Outside, the rain has settled into a drizzle and shows signs of stopping. I've decided to go for a walk in the wetlands. Good-bye, notebook! Good riddance!

▶ *E r i c*

It had been raining all afternoon, and I was running out of polite ways to tell Katie that I didn't want to play Barbies anymore. "Kate," I said, yawning, "it's homework time. How about if we park Barbie's car in the closet and sharpen our pencils?"

Katie was just a little first-grade kid with big green eyes and no homework. Her answer was the same every day. "Eerack," she said, "I did my homework when I got done with my regular seat work, after reading, before lunch." I made fish lips at her.

She sighed and sat her Barbies on the windowsill. I watched her line them up from my place on the edge of her bed.

Outside the window something beautiful happened. Julia Gagnon emerged from the front door of her house, pulled back the branch of a forsythia bush, and flung it at a tall, curly-mop guy who had followed her onto the porch.

"Water fight!" I told Katie. She looked out and watched in amazement as they shook branches on each other. It would have been a funny thing to catch on video.

"Can't we go out?" Katie said, whining, then shrugged, realizing she'd forgotten about my disability again. It was getting very boring, that broken leg.

"Let's try," I said, and she jumped up happily, surprised.

"There are puddles all over the road," I told her. "You'll have to help me along."

"Sure!" she said. Good kid. We got me down the stairs, pulled on our sweatshirts (it was too warm for coats), and opened our front door.

SCIENCE OBSERVATION

APRIL 16

Over Katie's head I saw Janine come stalking out her front door past her sister. As Janine turned onto the street, toward the wetlands, Julia nailed her in the face with a big, bouncy, wet branch. Julia's glossy hair was full of raindrops, and her cheeks were all roses. I couldn't hear her voice because Katie was saying something to me.

Janine didn't know whether to laugh or cry. She looked as though any change of weather at all might cause her face to crack.

She disappeared quickly down the street and turned onto the wetlands path. She was out of sight before Katie and I made it to our gate. Then we decided to head toward the wetlands, too.

There was no fear of catching up with Janine. Katie ran in circles around me while I hobbled along the bumpy road on my crutches. The afternoon light wouldn't start to die until six o'clock. The air smelled like sun and thunder all at once. As a meteorologist I look forward to storms. One thing I've learned from meteorology is that a little shake-up is good for all nature.

We didn't see Janine again at all, but I could still hear her sister laughing with that lucky guy, who didn't look like he deserved her.

That fisherman who often parked on our road went by, on his way to the pond. "Good day for it," he said.

"Yeah," I said. Good day for walking on crutches, is that what he meant? Sure, I thought, come trade places.

Mr. Lincoln, I know you wanted more interpretation from the class; I'm assuming I've done enough in that area so far and you didn't mean me. Just in case you're wondering, I think Janine is steamed that her sister has a boyfriend and she doesn't.

There's more, but Mom's yelling to me to come help with dinner.

JANINE

SCIENCE OBSERVATION
APRIL 17

I'm writing this down because it's what happened yesterday, and I've just sort of gotten used to writing lately. I've already done my assignment for this week. I'm not sure how far I'll get, but if I do—well, I'll deal with that when I come to it. I just ought to go get another notebook, but this one is handy. Well, here goes.

I saw that man again, the one who caught me wading. He has the straightest, shiniest dark brown hair I've ever seen, and a nice smile, too. I'll be honest, I've been thinking about him a lot, and more than a few times I've walked to the wetlands just because I hoped he'd be there. Interesting: I observed about myself that I was interested in an older man. So much for being immature, Miss Julia, Miss Barbara, Miss Kelly.

He actually got me to smile back at him again, which is something I didn't feel like doing after Julia added insult to injury by trying to get me involved in her romantic water fight. She looked so beautiful when I turned around to give her my evil scowl. There were raindrops on her eyelashes, and her eyes were glowing.

I had come outside in such a rush that I hadn't bothered to change into Jeff's boots. I never gave it a thought until I found myself sliding in my loafers across the muddy path that leads to the millpond. And then the fisherman was there in front of me. He laughed and said, "Don't you ever wear the appropriate thing on your feet?"

I couldn't believe he'd be joking with me—little me, big old him! It wasn't until he'd disappeared over the brow of the hill, walking toward the pond, that I noticed my heart beating and my face smiling. The sun was streaming through the clouds, and there were patches of blue sky.

I turned and walked along the ridge behind the brow of the hill. It's a big bluff, really, that slopes down on the other side toward the pond, with a good view of the old red millhouse that sits on top of a little waterfall. I felt embarrassed by the fisherman and didn't know why. I hadn't made him talk or smile at me, hadn't tried to get his attention the way Julia was trying to get Lionel's. I stayed on the ridge, which, if you know about it, is a great hiding place. Jeff and I used to come here and try to spy on people—fisherfolk or hikers—back when he took the time to do such things.

I wondered where the fisherman had gone, but I kept my head carefully below the edge of the bluff. The way I'd been slip-sliding around when he came along, he probably didn't know if I was coming or leaving. I'd planned to go to the pond to see if the water was warming up any, but now, if I did that, I would feel that I was following the fisherman. I sidestepped along the side of the hill, using my loafers like skis, and hid myself among a cluster of bushes and trees. I crept along behind the bushes and very, very slowly sneaked up until I could see over the brow of the hill and down to the pond. I just wanted to see him again, his gleaming hair, to look without being seen. Was it spying? I guess so. But I was just doing what Mr. Lincoln said, finding someone interesting.

[On a stapled-down sheet of paper]

MR. LINCOLN—DON'T READ!!!

The man was there, but he wasn't fishing. He was standing at the edge of the pond, where the spring ice had melted to dark, dark water. His fishing pole was in the white plastic bucket at his feet. At first I thought that his hands were in his pockets, that his elbows were shaking because he was cold. Then I saw what he had in his hands.

Julia says it's more mature to use anatomical terms, but all I can say in this case is *it*. What I mostly could see was his hands, shaking, rubbing. Then he peed, a little arc of spray into the pond. As I watched, he shook it, then peed into the pond. I put my hands over my mouth. At first I found it as funny as I would if I caught Jeff peeing in the backyard. Then I ducked as low as I could go and peered between the grass blades to make sure of what I'd seen. When he was done, he turned from the pond with his head down, and zipped up. And then— then he looked up toward me, looked exactly at the place where I was hiding, and smiled.

He couldn't see me. I knew he couldn't see me! I slid below the ridge and whirled away down the grassy back of the bluff, skidding on the slippery bottoms of my loafers. When I hit the path at the bottom, I ran, slipping and sliding, until I reached the road. I had the most horrible feeling in my stomach, as if I were the one caught doing something bad. When I got to the road, I stopped, panting, with my hand clutching my stomach.

Standing there on the road was Eric Gooch, crutches, video camera, and all. His little sister, Katie, the one with the long braids, who Julia baby-sits for, was climbing in the old snow at the side of the road. She didn't see me, but Eric stared as if I'd risen from the dead to walk out of that path.

"What happened?" he said, as if I were his little sister, not Katie.

"Nothing!" I answered, wishing he would disappear.

"Then what's the matter?" I was already five steps past him.

"What's the matter with *you*?" I yelled at him, and went home.

> ## *Eric*

When Katie and I reached the end of the street, after about a hundred years of what I loosely call walking, we almost bumped right into Janine. She was already coming back from the wetlands, not having stayed half as long as she usually did.

She was out of breath and her cheeks were red, and she looked like she wanted to hit somebody—Katie or me or anybody who was handy. Well, that wasn't so unusual in itself, but the freaky, upset look was.

Katie never even saw Janine pass, because right then she fell on her face in the mushy snowbank. I hauled her wet body out as well as I could, and we headed for home to dry off. Julia was standing at her gate. Her male friend was nowhere in sight. Neither was Janine.

"What happened, Katie?" Julia called, observing my sister's sopping clothes and runny nose. We took the excuse to walk across to the Gagnons' front door. Julia pulled a tissue from her jeans pocket and told Katie to blow, and while Katie was blowing, she made a motion with her head toward Janine's bedroom window.

"Did you say something to set her off?" she asked me.

"What? Me? No! But she sure looked weird when she went by."

"Yes," said Julia, shaking her head. "I worry about her. She's so lonesome lately."

"I think that's how she likes it," I said. "Besides, if anyone can take care of herself, it's Janine."

Julia considered that, then shrugged and went back inside.

☉ Janine

The next morning when I woke up, it seemed like a silly joke. Nothing had happened, after all. The man had just been peeing. What else could it have been? If I hadn't spotted him, nothing would have happened differently.

Why had I written it all down? If I pulled the pages out of my observation notebook, everything else would fall out, too. Cheap garbage! I had to go in and staple down the scary part. Then I added some words to the end of the other part that came before so Mr. Lincoln would just think I was looking for a new observation subject.

I couldn't stop thinking about what had happened, even though I'd covered up what I'd written. It made me sort of sick. That fisherman must have been some kind of weirdo, to smile when someone saw him. But then I remembered how sometimes my father forgot to close the bathroom door. If I said, "Hey, Daddy, I can see you," he'd just laugh and call back, "Hey, so what? I changed your diapers, you know!" But he hasn't let it happen lately.

So maybe the man *did* know I'd seen him. He must have been laughing because he was embarrassed, like Dad, not laughing at me. How could I have thought anything else?

I remembered something else, too. Once, in third grade, I tried climbing onto a toilet at school to see if I could see over the top of the stall and check who was in the bathroom. Not only did I get high enough to see Cynthia Dankowitz at the sink, but when I looked down sideways, I saw Barbara Finney's bare rear. She screamed, "Janine!" and jumped up, and I jumped down, and we met outside the stalls with very red faces.

"I was just climbing around," I said, refusing to apologize.

"Oh, sure!" she said. "Well, *don't!*"

After that she was especially nice to me. I figured she was afraid not to be, because I might tell what I'd seen. It was one of the reasons we're friends—that, plus the fact that she didn't know I'd told Artie and Kelly.

That's how it would be with the fisherman, I told myself. If I saw him again—and I hoped I did not—he would pretend he'd never seen me before in his life.

I was through thinking about him and his idiotic shiny hair, through following him around the wetlands, hoping to see his pink cheeks.

It was useless to change the subject on myself, though. Because I kept seeing that smile. There was a big difference between the kind of laugh I just described and the smile I saw yesterday. He was happy I saw him. He was feeling good and was glad to have me see him doing it. Why, I'm not sure, but that's what was happening to him.

What was happening to me? Now that was a different story. Because now I felt like I didn't have anywhere to go. Couldn't escape and go to the wetlands; he might be there. I didn't intend to dwell on what happened yesterday. But I didn't want it to happen again, either.

I made up my mind right then and there how I would think of it: He didn't do anything to me. He was just *over there,* at a distance, doing something. He could have been setting his line, tying his shoe, brushing his hair out of his eyes. It didn't have anything to do with me. There wasn't anything to be concerned about.

A little itch of annoyance was still with me: Eric Gooch. What had he been doing there, lurking around where he had seen me last? Who did he think he was, staring at me that bug-eyed way? Why did he ask me, "What happened?" What made him think anything had happened? Nothing had happened. Nothing at all.

Chapter 6

*J*anine directs her gaze upward, at the straight dark hair, and she makes herself think of Artie O'Halloran. Artie O'Halloran has blond hair that was almost white when he came back from Cape Cod last summer, and his skin was so brown and his eyes were so blue, back then. They are the bluest eyes, blue like the little stopper in the end of a ballpoint pen.

Artie is small, as small as she is, and strong like her but with bigger muscles. It doesn't mean anything, having muscles. It's just something boys get as they get older, that and—

What Janine wishes she were doing is watching Artie O'Halloran play baseball. When he's at shortstop, he stands hunched over, his knees slightly bent, his hands dangling nearly to the ground. Artie is loose, still, ready to go left or right, backward or forward. When Janine is playing second, hanging close to her base, she tries to match Artie move for move. Spry and graceful, that's Janine, as much on the ballfield as on the dance floor. She turns that double play every time. She can see the play in her mind as clearly as the leaves on the trees that edge the pond: Artie fields the grounder and flips it to her. She steps on second and whirls

*to fling the ball to first. The umpire's elbow bends: "Out!"
She looks over at Artie and smiles.*

*The image of Artie's blond hair blurs, and there in his
place is the fisherman. Magnetic. Repulsive. She moves
toward him on the balls of her bare feet, ready to spring, to
spin, to go left or right as the game demands. His eyes are
focused on her, but his body shows a different readiness.
He's centered on himself, on the part of him that is just
below center. He's selfish, she realizes. She would have been
content just to look at him, knowing, really, that she is too
young to touch his lovely hair or his broad shoulders or any
other part of him.*

*He should have just looked, too, should have understood
that he was too old. He shouldn't have to unzip his pants and
stand there showing her all there is. He shouldn't need to
reach across the gap between them, to try to hurt her and
embarrass her, to make her want to go home and cry and
cry. It isn't working, thinking about Artie, thinking that men
are just large versions of boys. It isn't working.*

Feet, turn away and take me with you.

Get me away from him.

Get me away from here.

*Just do this one thing and I'll dance with anybody: Clark
Jamison, Eric Gooch. No matter how much of a dweeb he is,
I'll dance.*

✿ *Janine*

"Eric's got a crush on Julia, Mother," I said to the back of her head. She was rushing us up the drive of the Tattersall Club. She was catering the annual dinner of the Board of Realtors, Mrs. Gooch included, and she was in a state. When Mother failed to respond, I added, "Isn't that sweet?"

"Don't be snide, Janine," she said quickly. "It's so unattractive." Did she think I was trying to attract anyone?

Eric snorted and looked out the window, his face red behind his glasses, his hand on the door handle, ready to spring. "Have fuh-un!" Mother sang out, and flipped the electric lock switch as though she wished it were an ejector button.

But before we even got our doors open, Kelly Kim's mother came fluttering and flapping up to the car.

"Oh, Yvonne, did you hear?" she burst out. "Poor little Charlie!"

Mother put the car in park and looked blankly at Mrs. Kim.

"He's in the hospital, just this afternoon."

"Why?" asked the Gooch.

"Oh, honey, do *you* know Charlie, too? I didn't realize— Oh, but of course! You're the little Gooch boy, back *home* now, aren't you?" The little Gooch boy. I filed that away for future use.

"Ginny, go on!" Mother said sharply. "*What* about Charlie?"

"He'll be okay, but aw, the poor kid. He was cooking spaghetti for his mother and carrying the pot of boiling water to the sink. Well, one of the kids must have dropped butter on the floor, and Charlie slipped."

My mother pulled up the emergency brake and sat with

91

her face in her hands. Mrs. Kim subsided and said quietly, "Third-degree burns on his chest and arms."

"Oh, *man*," said Gooch, and took off up the path on his own, looking shaken.

I followed, after closing both car doors. But Mother opened her door and called me back. "Just to give you a hug," she said.

I went up the steps slowly. Charlie Panucci was not my favorite person, but it wasn't good to think of anyone pouring hot, boiling spaghetti water all down his front.

Without a word I held Eric's crutches while he took off his coat. "Thank you," he said, and looked at my face. His eyes behind his glasses were enormous and green. I shrugged, shaken, and walked away.

I went to stand with Barbara and Susan and Kelly, who were buzzing about Charlie. "We could make him a giant card tomorrow in Art," said Barbara, her blue eyes bright and eager. "Mrs. Shadner will let us. We can use the big paper roll for cheerleading banners—"

"And get everyone to sign it," added Kelly, on hand to finish Barbara's sentences, as usual.

Susan, who spoke her own sentences, if she spoke, played nervously with the ends of her fluffy blond hair. "Who's going to take it to him?" she wondered.

Nobody volunteered. We all were picturing walking into a hospital room and seeing Charlie Panucci in the bed. No, thank you.

Then Marcy Moreno leaned into our circle and said, "I'll take it if you're nervous. I've already seen him."

"You have? Why?" Barbara's mouth was a big pink O. She hates anybody to do anything first.

"I was there, kind of."

"Oh, sure," I said.

Big-eyed Susan would have liked to take a step back but

didn't. "I *was*, Janine," Marcy said. "His brother, Anthony, ran over to my house when it happened and got me to stay with them all when the ambulance came."

"Ambulance!" It was funny I hadn't heard any siren. Jeff's music again.

"What was it like?" Susan asked softly.

Marcy's pond-colored eyes blinked back tears. How unbelievably dramatic.

"You're not going to cry, are you?" I asked, leaning toward her.

"What if I did, Janine?" She pushed her face closer to mine.

"You should go, Marcy," said Kelly. Who did Kelly think she was? Did she have a secret crush on Charlie perhaps, more secret than Marcy's?

"He was in pain," said Marcy, standing straight again.

"A lot?" from Susan.

Marcy nodded.

"Crying?" from Kelly.

Nodded again.

Everyone was silent. Then: "I'll get the paint from Mr. Lincoln," said Barbara. "Sue, can you . . ."

So Marcy was elected the messenger and admitted to the in group, all in one evening.

> *Eric*

With Charlie missing, there was one girl odd at dancing school, and whoever was left over was told to come sit with me.

This idea made me nervous until I realized that the leftover girl would be an unchosen one. I wasn't likely to sit dances out with Kelly Kim, not in this lifetime.

First, it was Cynthia Dankowitz, and it was a tango. She didn't have anything much to say. She had pimples and thin blond hair and a very quiet personality, except for those times that she'd stuck up for Marcy. Finally, "Did you hear about Charlie?" she said, desperate for something to say.

"Hasn't everybody?"

"Third-degree burns!" she said.

"What does that mean exactly?" I said, not wanting to hear.

"Really bad," she answered. "First degree is sunburn. Second degree is blisters. Third degree is burned skin."

"Stop!" I said. My eyes were watering, for Charlie's sake.

"Are you okay?" she asked, bending to look into my face. Smart *and* sensitive; too bad about her looks.

"Yeah," I said. "He's a good friend, that's all."

"Well, I don't think anybody really knows," she said. "People like to spread the worst news possible."

Well, that was an interesting observation.

Out on the floor Janine was tangoing with Jerry Sutter, a non-honors, jock-looking kid, and didn't seem pleased about it. Artie O'Halloran was dancing with Susan Hackman, and did. But the look on Janine's face could scald—

Don't think about it, I told myself.

⊚ Janine

It was hot, steaming hot, in the Tattersall Club, and Miss Seal appealed to her mother to open the French doors at snack break. I went and sat with Barbara and Susan and managed to plant the idea in Susan's head to ask Mrs. Seal for a Sadie Hawkins dance (when girls ask boys) after break. I gave her the idea that this way girls could grab Charlie's friends and consult them about the card giving.

So that's how it happened.

I walked, I did not run, across the floor and straight into Artie O'Halloran's arms. Well, not exactly, but into his eyes, which met mine almost immediately and never left me as I moved steadily toward him.

"Dance?" I said as if I didn't care. He stood up and took my hand, and before long we were fox-trotting. I got him talking about hockey, and he asked me about Jeff, and we had a real conversation, although he didn't seem much interested in listening to *me*. All too soon the song was over. But Mrs. Seal was clapping her hands.

"Freeze!" she said. "Freeze, all!" I rolled my eyes at Artie, and he actually smiled. Hmm, I thought, but I didn't get the chance to say something funny about Mrs. Seal because she was making a speech.

"Now, perhaps we should do this the other way around, because a fox usually chases a rabbit." She waited. No one had any idea what she was talking about. "If you all will find seats—yes, keep the *same* partners [gosh, I was blessed!]—Mr. Bert and Miss Seal will instruct you in"—pause for effect—"the bunny hop!"

I groaned, and Artie grinned. We sat down in front of the French doors, next to Barbara and her partner, Artie's friend Jerry Sutter. Jerry is cute, with light brown hair and freckles, but not as cute as Artie. We all rocked on our chairs and whispered back and forth, while out on the floor Bert and Miss Seal demonstrated the stupidest dance known to the human race. We were actually supposed to shake our cottontails and hop like bunnies, with our hands on each other's hips.

"Sappy bunnies," said Jerry. We all giggled and rocked our chairs, just a little, so Mrs. Seal wouldn't see.

"Hoppy, sappy bunnies." Barbara laughed. Artie and I grinned, but not at each other. It would be fun to make him laugh at me.

"This is the dumbest thing I've ever heard of," said Artie. We giggled, and I tried again to think of something funny.

"No, the stupidest thing I've ever heard is about Charlie Panucci," I said.

"Oh, yeah?" said Artie. Jerry and Barbara leaned in to hear what I was going to say. Suddenly I saw myself as though from a distance, sitting with the boy I liked and his cute best friend, and Barbara Finney, the girl everyone most wanted to sit with at lunch.

"Yeah!" I said. "Can you imagine being stupid enough to pour hot, boiling spaghetti water all over yourself?" And I laughed a lot louder than any of us had laughed over the bunny hop.

"Janine!" scolded Barbara, sounding as prissy as Miss Seal.

Artie's face turned red. "That's just the kind of thing I'd expect you to say, Janine," he whispered, as though he didn't trust himself to speak at a normal level.

"Yeah," said Jerry. He nudged Artie's arm. "You were right about what you told me about her," he added. And Artie and Jerry rocked their chairs back, way back. Together they tipped their chairs backward, fell out the French doors, and ran away onto the warm, dark golf course.

It was just as everyone was getting up to try the bunny

hop. Barbara walked right up to Susan, and I heard her say in a loud voice, "You know what Janine Gagnon said about Charlie?"

▶ *Eric*

"Where's your mother?" Janine had me by the sleeve.

I shrugged her hand away. "Where do you think?" Mom was just where she was supposed to be, standing in the vestibule with the other parents, even though she'd had to leave the Board of Realtors dinner to get here.

All the parents were talking about Charlie. People don't know when to shut up. The trouble was that Mom didn't know any of these parents, since I was new to school, except the Gagnons and the Panuccis, who weren't there. So, in the car, she naturally wanted to know all about what had happened to Charlie. Janine didn't say a word. She sat in the front seat and looked straight ahead.

"He got burned, Mom, all right?" I said. "He was boiling water for spaghetti, and he slipped."

Mom gasped. "But why—"

"Do we *have* to talk about it?" asked Janine. She wasn't rude or anything, just strained, like she wanted to scream, and Mom glanced back at me where I sat in the back behind Janine, with my leg stretched across the seat.

"Well," Mom said. "Well, Janine, do you cook?"

I could see where this was going. Mom wasn't exactly used to the idea of a thirteen-year-old cooking spaghetti.

"My mother is a Cordon Bleu cook," Janine said stiffly.

"We all have our specialties." Hers was probably something in a cauldron.

Mom tried to be pleasant. "It's a good idea to learn all the life skills you can."

"That's just what I told Dad about wilderness camp," I said, seeing a chance to change the subject. "Everybody needs basic survival skills."

"It depends on how you define *survival*," my mother said.

"Would you say dancing school was a life skill?" Janine asked, still staring out the window.

"Some people would say—" Mom answered, but I was still pursuing my opportunity.

"Survival skills like knowing how to stay warm in the woods, or how to defend yourself from an animal attack, or what to eat if you're out of food, or how to make a shelter—"

"What are you talking about?" Janine sounded more like her normal self.

"Wilderness college!" I announced, leaning forward. "You didn't know? I'm going this summer."

"Eric," my mother said, but I interrupted again.

"In Canada," I said. "Eight weeks. Canoeing, hiking, survival—"

"You're going to wildlife camp?" Janine said eagerly. "Maybe I— Where is it?"

"Wilderness," I corrected her.

"Eric, that decision has not been made."

"I think it has," I said. "I'm not going to golf camp for a million dollars, Mom. I don't care what he says."

We were on Kingfisher Lane now, pulling into our driveway.

"This isn't the time or place," Mom said.

Janine opened the door of the car the instant it stopped.

"Thanks for the ride," she said to my mother.

To me she said, "Golf camp?" I made a face. She was making the same face. We were both crossing our eyes and twisting our mouths, and it was almost funny except that of course she was making fun of me.

Charlie, I thought, and straightened out my face as I hoisted myself out of the backseat. Janine was already gone, across the street and through her gate.

Mom was in the kitchen talking to Julia, but even the prospect of seeing that pretty face couldn't lure me away from the prospect of sleep. Suddenly the whole night was just too much for me.

At the top of the stairs I stopped to get my breath, and there was Katie, sound asleep in her bed. Across the street Janine's light was on in her room. I thought about Charlie, wondered where he was and how he was doing. As I watched, Julia went out our door and crossed the street, her dark hair shining as she passed under the light.

"Eric?" my mother whispered loudly up the stairs as she was on the way up. In my room I sat on the bed to take my one shoe off. Mom came in and moved my crutches to the side of my bed for me.

"Did anyone say what happened to Charlie after he spilled the water?" she asked.

I felt a shudder creep up my shoulders and tried to keep it from showing, but Mom saw. She sat down beside me on the bed and rubbed my shoulders. She looked tired and anxious, her brown hair escaping as always from its ponytail. It was a long day for her, working and going to school and realtors' dinners and driving Katie and me around.

"They took him to the hospital," I said. "That's all anybody knows."

She looked at her watch. "Too late now to call over there," she said. "Besides—"

"About that survival camp," I said. "I'm going, all right?"

She gave me a steady look before answering. "I can't even begin to name the *ifs*," she said.

"*If* my leg is good enough by then," I said.

"That's not the half of it, and you know it."

"If you think I'm going to golf camp—"

"Eric," she said in a voice that should have stopped me, "this is not the time to make waves."

"What waves?" I asked. I could be just as pigheaded as my parents. "Mom, I'm in this lousy school, aren't I? I'm making the best of things here. Why can't—"

"It's not a lousy school," my mother said tiredly. "I think you're a little bit of a snob, Eric. In any case, it's true: You *are* at a disadvantage right now. It's a difficult time. You're going to have to swallow it for the time being, make some concessions."

Concessions! I swung my leg onto the bed, wishing she would leave so I could put my pajamas on. I turned onto my side gingerly and said to the wall, "I want to go to wilderness college. If I have to be here and go to this school, I ought to be able to go to the camp I choose."

I expected to hear her get up and walk away and leave me alone then, but that just goes to show how well I didn't know my own mother. "You ought to, Eric?" she asked, shaking my shoulder. I turned onto my back and looked at her, saw anger I'd never seen her show to anyone but Dad. "There are a lot of things we all *ought* to be able to do," she said. "Do yourself a favor. Don't expect anything to be fair right now."

"Does that mean I'm staying at this school?" I asked. I figured I might as well find out now as later. "Just tell me right now." Make this awful night complete.

Mom sat there looking down at me, and all of a sudden it came back to me, what it had been like to be at home all the time and have her tuck me in bed at night, the way she did with Katie. It occurred to me that it was very highly likely that I would still be here a year from now, riding the bus to Marsh Park High School with Janine and Jeff, instead of Haycock Senior School.

For a second I wondered who would room with Pete, and whether Dad would like the college I'd get into with a diploma from Marsh Park, and whether I'd ever be my regular self, ever again.

"Is that what Dad wants me to do?" I sat up angrily and stared at Mom's face. She still hadn't said a word. She sat there and looked at me with such a sad expression that I bit back the words I was about to spit out.

"I haven't been privileged to receive any information about your father's desires," she said formally, standing up. "Only yours. And I'm hearing them loud and clear, Eric." She left my room, and tired though I was, I couldn't sleep for a long time.

Chapter 7

*K*atie walks along Henry Street holding the open umbrella, wishing the wind would pick up so she can find out if the umbrella will carry her along, like Mary Poppins. But wait, Mary Poppins came on the east wind. Katie stops and figures out where the sun would be if the clouds weren't so thick. Over there, that must be west. She licks a finger and holds it up into the wind the way Eric taught her. "West," she says aloud. She sighs and continues walking to Amy Panucci's house.

When she gets there, Amy's mother's van is gone. The lights are on, though. Only Amy's big brother Charlie is home. Katie likes Charlie; he's good at playing monster with her and Amy, and he likes doing Lego as much as they do. She's glad her brother has made friends with Charlie.

"Are you sure you're supposed to come here?" Charlie asks her in his friendly way. He talks to her as if she's grown up. "Amy's at the dentist."

"Julia Gagnon told me."

"Julia?" Katie knows it's sort of strange, but lately she's gotten used to all kinds of people letting her know where she should be and who's taking care of her.

She tells him, "Eric's at the wetlands. He's taking pictures *of the clouds. But it's going to rain. Eric said so, and he knows all about the weather. So he sent me to get Julia to bring him an umbrella."*

"But you're here with the umbrella," says Charlie, puzzled.

"Julia sent me here with this one, and she took another one to Eric."

"She took it to him?"

"Right. He's at the wetlands. He's videoing."

"Videoing what? Is something going on?"

"No," says Katie. "It's just the weather changing."

Charlie looks out the window, then bends slowly to put on his sneakers. He's as creaky as Eric, and she tells him so. "Yeah." He laughs. "We're a couple of sickies." Then he picks up an umbrella of his own and opens the door. "Let's go find your brother," he says. They walk slowly to the wetlands the Henry Street way, talking about who lives in the houses: which people, which cats, which dogs.

JANINE

SCIENCE OBSERVATION
APRIL 20

Why didn't they laugh?
    If only they'd laughed.
    If only they hadn't run away to squeal to everyone about what I'd said.

They were worse than dweebs. They were a bunch of retards.

Why couldn't they just have laughed?

The next day I made Julia drive me to school early, even though it meant missing out on her early-morning "editorial meeting" with Lionel. I told her if she didn't, I would tell Mother what those editorial meetings really are, a chance to make out.

I walked through the still-empty hallways and found a chair behind a shelf in the library. I curled up there to write this observation.

This is my plan: to ignore Clark Jamison and Kelly Kim and Marcy Moreno and Eric Gooch and Barbara Finney—but especially, most especially, Artie O'Halloran.

That's what I'm doing still, in Whole Learning, while the classroom is filling up. I'm behind in my science observations, anyway. Now I'm going wild writing. I'm even writing about what happened at dancing school, and I don't even know why. It makes me sick to think about it, so why write it? It serves its purpose. I've discovered that when you look occupied, people don't think you're listening.

Right behind me I heard Clark whisper to Artie, "So what happened when they caught *you*?" I didn't hear Artie's answer, but I smiled to myself. Ha. Good. Artie and Jerry had gotten in trouble for running away. I had reported them to Mrs. Seal, of course, when Barbara took off, pretending she had to go to the girls' room. That weird man teacher, Bert, found Jerry in the bushes out front of the Tattersall. But when Eric's mother arrived to pick us up, Artie had not yet turned up. They probably figured it was me who told. Well, of course I did. How could I let them get away with what they did to me, them and their big mouths?

It's lunch now. I heard Marcy ask Eric to go with her to the hospital to see Charlie Panucci. "He's your friend, too," she said. "He's been so nice to both of us"—Charlie Panucci, nice? Where, at the bus stop? That sap!—"and my mom's going to pick me up, so if you want to ride with us . . ."

When I heard Eric accept, I silently celebrated, all the while scribbling in my green book. With him and Marcy getting a ride from school, I can ride the bus home in peace.

Later

Then, on the bus, I kicked myself. Why couldn't I ride in peace *with* them on the bus? What kind of jellyfish was I, anyway? All I said was—

Then I remembered what I'd said about Charlie Panucci. I remembered the way Artie's and Barbara's faces looked when I said it. So what if Eric and Marcy *did* hear about it? I imagine what their faces looked like when they heard. And now they're going to see Charlie.

Well, who cares? What if they *do* tell Charlie what I said? What if Jerry does, or Artie, or anyone else?

My neck grew hot and prickly, my face must certainly

have turned red, and my eyes began— I leaped out of my seat and jumped off the bus two stops early. I swung my backpack over my shoulder and walked quickly down the street, blinking tears.

I, Janine Gagnon, was embarrassed. I had made fun of somebody everyone else likes, who was hurt even, and they were all angry about it. All day, while I sat writing, I thought I was shutting everyone out. Now it occurs to me that no one had even tried to get my attention. Not one person came near me or talked to me or wrote me a note. Teachers called on me, I answered, and that was all.

It makes me furious! All I did was say something perfectly true about Charlie the dweeb Panucci, who gets all the kids to come to his bus stop while I stand there all alone at mine.

But a picture somehow poked in on my angry thoughts as I walked by Charlie's house, which looked dark and empty, its lights off, door closed, cars gone. In my mind's eye I saw boiling water falling over Charlie, and I could only imagine what came afterward. I thought about Marcy telling the girls about Charlie last night, about saying to her, "You're not going to cry, are you?" Nearly home now, I recalled what I'd said about Charlie, my exact words: "Can you imagine being stupid enough to pour hot, boiling spaghetti water all over yourself?" Again my eyes filled with tears, and I bit back a sob. Why didn't they laugh? They didn't laugh because it wasn't funny.

► *Eric*

I was in the school cafeteria eating chili and studying the weather map in the morning newspaper when Marcy Moreno pulled up a chair beside me. Susan Hackman stood behind Marcy with a big scroll of art paper clutched in her hands. Susan had silver rings on her fingers and dangling blue earrings under curly blond hair. Pretty. Kelly Kim came along to join them, wearing a red sweater that was enough to give me the shivers. They were on a mission.

"It's about Charlie," Marcy said. She looked intently at me with troubled green-brown eyes. "I talked to his mother this morning. Second-degree burns, not third." I just looked at her, gulping like a fish.

Susan said, "That means blisters." I felt sick.

Marcy looked as if she knew what I was feeling. "We got everyone to sign this card," she said.

"Almost everyone," said Kelly, and lowered her voice. "Did you hear what Janine said about him?"

"Yeah," I said, shaking my head. "Telegraph, telephone, and tell Artie."

Kelly's shoulders dropped. "Well, Artie is Charlie's friend, too, you know!"

"But maybe you're Janine's friend?" whispered Susan. "You *do* ride the bus together and drive to dancing school."

I looked away and said quietly, "She's right over there, you know." I pointed a finger left, and there was Janine at the next table, ears apparently closed to everyone around her, scribbling away in her green science notebook. What could she be observing in here?

In a voice loud enough to be heard three tables away, Marcy announced, "Eric, I'm going to see Charlie today. My mother's picking me up. Maybe—since you're sort of disabled?—we could give you a ride. You could present our class card to Charlie with me."

"Well, okay," I said, glancing at Janine. She was writing faster than ever. About what? About who? One of us? "Okay!" I said again, louder this time. "I'd be glad to avoid the bus ride home."

JANINE

[Written in an old blue notebook]
SCIENCE OBSERVATION
APRIL 23

Mr. Lincoln, I don't want to observe myself anymore. I met somebody interesting today. Her name is Kathleen; it's on a necklace she was wearing when I met her. I was wading in the water at the pond. It is still pretty cold down there. Grass is growing on the bottom, new light green grass mixing with slimy brown last-year grass.

I was farther out than I'd ever been before, halfway across the little cove beside the mill. I focused my eyes on the surface of the water, watching rings grow out from my fingers.

"Hey, girl!" came a squawk from the other side of the little cove. A woman appeared, nearly camouflaged by the tall tan reeds. Her hair and her shirt and her jeans and her skin were all brown. Her eyes were clear and sharp like she was always outside, and she was spitting angry.

She said, "Don't you know you're killing fish?"

I said, "Me?"

"Ten thousand tiny fish eggs in every step. Fish! Frogs! Turtles!"

"In the mud?"

She thought I was an idiot. "Of course in the mud! What do you think mud is for? The primordial ooze from which life is formed? The perfect medium for birth and growth?"

I had never thought about it, but it seemed it probably was true.

"Walk this way; then go around the edge," she ordered me.

I walked and tried to say something to give her a clue that I had brain cells working. "So this pond, it's like one big nursery?"

"That's right," she said. "Don't stomp!"

"But how do you *know*?" I asked.

"I've made a study of it."

She has just moved into the decrepit old mill. Says the university borrowed it from the town so she could make a study.

This is the great part. I asked her, "What do you have to do?"

"I'm taking a lot of samples right now. Seeing what's there. Seeing what grows."

"Samples of what?" I asked.

She answered, "Eggs. Water. Ooze." She smiled. She'd decided to let me live. "I've got them on slides under a microscope inside. I'm doing a population study of the whole pond."

I'm going back to see her tomorrow.

Mr. Lincoln, is it too late to change my observation subject? Say I can and I'll try at least to find out her last name.

▶ *Eric*

After school Mrs. Moreno, a short, round lady, drove Marcy and me to the hospital in her old Volkswagen. As we turned into the parking lot, it occurred to me that this morning Mom had knocked on the bathroom door while I was brushing my teeth to ask me to come right home from school to be with Katie. She was taking some real-estate test and wouldn't be home until six.

I sat up straight in alarm, and Marcy said, "Something wrong?"

"I'm supposed to be home," I moaned. "My sister— I just remembered."

"There'll be a phone inside," Mrs. Moreno said.

"We'll go on up," said Marcy. "Mom, what room is it?"

My mind leaped to Charlie, as it had several times this afternoon at school: What would he look like? Was he in pain? Would he be awake? Would he have tubes . . . ?

"I'll call," I said.

The phone was around a corner, in a little nook by a window that looked out on the sunny spring afternoon. I didn't feel sunny inside, thinking of Charlie, thinking of Katie, and I felt even worse as I listened to our house phone ring and ring, imagining it in the empty kitchen. Where was Katie?

I hung up and dialed the Gagnons' number. Julia answered on the second ring. I could hear Jeff's loud music in the background. She put her hand over the phone and yelled, "Turn it down!" To me she said calmly, "We only just got home. She must have missed us. I'll go find her now, Eric. You go on and see Charlie. Don't worry, she must have gone to a neighbor's house."

"Thanks! I'll call back as soon as—"

But Julia had already hung up her phone to go find Katie.

I checked the pass the guard had given me and pressed the elevator button for the sixth floor. I felt silly, thinking of Charlie, real Charlie fooling around in my living room, talking about girls, not lying sick and hurt somewhere—

Not somewhere. Here. Down this hall, through this door, inside this room, in that bed.

"Eric's here, Charlie!" Mrs. Panucci (an older, fatter, female version of Charlie) took my arm and pulled me closer, crutches and all. Charlie looked terrible. His curly hair was every which way, his face was pale and strained. There was a tube taped into his arm. He looked drowsy ("sedated," whispered Marcy).

"Check me out, Gooch," he said in a low voice. "The spaghetti king."

"Yeah, too bad the snow melted," I said, matching his tone. "We could take you out and roll you in it."

Marcy gulped a little, and her mother said, "Marcy, why don't you ask the nurses for some Scotch tape? You could put up that card." Marcy didn't look like she wanted to leave the room, but she went.

She came back with a roll of tape and went to work taping the card to the wall, where Charlie could see it.

"Looks like everyone signed." Charlie raised an arm toward the poster. It seemed to hurt him to do it.

Everyone but one, I thought.

"Now, look, Charlie," Marcy said, not facing him but concentrating on the tape. "You'll be missing an awful lot of dancing school."

"What a tragedy," said Charlie slowly.

"Sure," I said. "Miss Seal will have to give you a private makeup lesson." Mrs. Moreno rolled her eyes at Mrs. Panucci as Charlie raised his eyebrows a couple of times.

"Mrs. Seal would do it better," said Marcy. "She'd be the first to say so."

We all laughed. Marcy had a way of laughing at people without being mean. Maybe it was because her mother was not the type to mind if kids ragged on adults sometimes. Or maybe it was just the circumstances, poor old Charlie all bandaged up in bed and trying to act cheerful, despite obviously feeling like he'd dumped six pots of boiling water on his chest, not just one.

"Well, I'm the best tutor of all when it comes to dancing school," I said, banging my cast with my crutch. I quoted Mr. Lincoln: " 'Observation is the best teacher,' you know?"

There were things Charlie would have liked to say if Marcy and the mothers hadn't been there. What he said was, "Video! That's the answer! You can video dancing school, and I'll watch. I won't miss a thing!"

"My goodness," said Mrs. Moreno, "I didn't know you boys were such devoted students." I knew what Charlie was thinking: Miss Seal, Kelly Kim, etc., on video. Plus Janine chasing Artie, and Bert doing the bunny hop, and other horrors. It would be prime entertainment. I was going to have to get some new tapes if I was going to keep up (filmwise) with dancing school, gym class, and Mean Janine, not to mention the weather. This spring was turning out to be the most productive period of my video career.

⊘ Janine

I had been stomping on fish eggs. That was bad of me, but . . .

I had a new observation subject. So I had a smile on my face. I stood on the muddy shore of the pond, feeling pretty good. For about two seconds.

Then I saw the fisherman, far away at the other end of the pond where the river flowed in. At the same moment I heard someone call my name.

"Janine!" It wasn't him. It was Katie Gooch, calling from the end of the path, at the water's edge, wading in her red boots into the primordial ooze. Her braids were blowing in the wind. She looked small and alone.

"I've been looking for you!" she cried. "I couldn't find anybody! Eric didn't come home. And there's nobody at your house."

I just stood there for a moment, not getting it at all. What did Katie want from me?

"Can I stay here with you?" Katie said.

"Where's your mother?"

"She's— She had to go somewhere, and Eric was supposed to be here."

I expected her to start crying, and she looked like she wanted to, but she didn't, and I had some respect for that.

"I know where Eric is," I said. "He went to see Charlie Panucci." I wondered if she thought I was friends with them or if she knew better.

"At his house?" I could see that Katie was thinking she should have gone to the Panuccis'. I was thinking about her walking all the way here by herself.

"How did you know where I was?" I asked.

"You're always here," she said. Funny she had noticed.

I knew how Katie must have felt when she came home and found nobody there. She must have been worried, but she hadn't just stood there and cried; she'd tried to solve her problem, and she'd thought of me.

I reached down and took Katie's hand. "It's okay now," I said. "*I'm* here. And I want to tell you something about the pond. But first, didn't Eric tell you what happened to Charlie?"

I told her about it as we walked along the path and up Kingfisher Lane, as plainly as possible. Her face as she listened was stoic and sad. "Did it hurt a lot?" she asked, looking up into my eyes.

"I think so," I said.

"Does it hurt him still now?"

"He's in the hospital," I answered. "Eric went to find out."

Katie thought about it for a minute. She said, "He didn't mean to forget me. He was worried about Charlie." I nodded. Just like that, she had told herself what she needed to know in order to feel better. And now she did. I was glad life was that simple for someone. Then she said, "I'm hungry." I stopped and took off my backpack, pulled out my box of raisins from lunch. We walked home along our road, eating raisins.

"I'm going to make a get-well card for Charlie," Katie

announced. Me, too, I thought. Now *that* would take some nerve.

Then Julia and Eric came hurrying up the street to meet us. That was when the good part of my day ended.

"Where have you been?" Eric roared. "And what have you been doing with Katie? Have you been in the pond? Couldn't you have left a note? What were we supposed to think? Didn't you think we—" It was the most he'd ever said to me.

"Oh, sure," I snapped back. "You've got a lot of nerve. Like you're Mr. Responsible, right? Where were *you*?"

▶ *Eric*

I stood there in the Gagnons' kitchen like the dweeb Janine always said I was, with both Katie and Julia staring at me. If only I hadn't gone to see Charlie. If only Charlie hadn't spilled the spaghetti water. If only I hadn't forgotten about Katie.

"Janine's nice," said Katie, the little traitor.

"Of course she is," said Julia. "And she's upstairs crying." I could hear the shower running.

"I'd never believe she could," I said coldly.

"Then you don't understand her at all," Julia said, just as coldly.

I had never heard her speak like that to anyone, and I recoiled a little. Katie was watching me.

"I'm hungry," said Katie, with all the manners of Mini Pearl.

"Want a Scooter Pie?" Julia looked at me and sighed. "I'm going to make some almond tea, too."

"Thanks," I said. Julia smiled. I dropped into a chair, feeling completely worn out. The kitchen was one of those chrome and white wood situations with an island in the middle that had nothing on it but a red geranium plant. In the window, herb plants were growing. They had handwritten labels: rosemary, oregano, basil. There was a watering schedule with Janine's and Jeff's and Julia's names on it. In the mudroom, visible through a doorway, a lot of what Janine would call jock stuff—sweatshirts hanging on hooks, jogging shoes, roller skates, hockey sticks (by next winter I'm going to learn to skate, I swear), and so on. Janine's and Jeff's, I guessed. Janine's schoolbooks, neatly covered and labeled, were dumped all over the counter.

Katie said, "Is there paper? Can I draw?" And she sat there coloring, telling me about the roller-skating party at school. I sat waiting for tea, which I didn't really want. But it was good to be sitting near Julia.

"Amy Panucci is scared of Janine," Katie said, "but I'm not."

Julia and I looked at each other. "Her bark is worse than her bite," Julia said.

"At least you admit she barks," I answered.

Julia shrugged. "She's got a strong personality. That's what my mother says. My father says she'll be president of something someday since she always knows what she wants."

I thought of Artie and shook my head. "She doesn't understand people," I said.

Julia had her back to me, getting out the tea bags and milk and things. If only Janine could be more like her sister. Julia must have thought she needed to stick up for Janine no matter what. I wondered what would have to happen before *Janine* stuck up for anyone. Then I realized Janine had stuck up for Katie. She had tried to help her out, anyway, which was the same thing.

I watched Julia reach into cupboards and the refrigerator,

117

watched her hair fall over her shoulder, and thought her long-sleeved maroon T-shirt was just the right thing for her to be wearing. I couldn't think of a single thing to say to her. I realized I might have some problems understanding people myself.

If I couldn't understand Janine after all these months of observation, was there something wrong with me? I don't think she would have helped Katie a month ago. She would have been more likely to stomp her lunch just to get at me. So had something happened? And if something had happened, what was it?

When it came right down to it, I was better at reading the clouds than I was at reading people. Yes, I should have gotten an A for even attempting to study Janine Gagnon, never mind understand her. Maybe instead of trying to read Janine, I should try to get a peek at whatever it is she's been writing ever since the night Charlie got burned.

When Katie got up to use the bathroom and Julia went to the pantry for the Scooter Pies, I made a quick decision to see for myself what was inside Janine Gagnon's head. I snatched her green science observation notebook from the counter and stuffed it inside my shirt. It lay cool and hard against my stomach. Good. So it was a crime against privacy. So it was spying. I didn't care.

I remembered when I'd thought observing Janine would be as boring as good weather. But if there's one thing I *should* have learned from meteorology, it's that boredom is deceptive. There's always something lurking around if you're just able to wait for it and see it when it starts.

Katie and Julia came back. The notebook grew warm against my skin. It was spying, no question about it.

Chapter 8

Marcy had an idea what this summer was going to be like with Kathleen here. Quiet. Good. The hot blue sky, cool mud between their toes, nets to splash each other with when they got too sweaty: It was going to be great. It didn't matter that her aunt Kathleen was so much older, did it? Or did it?

Marcy sighed. Already Kathleen spent a lot of time away from the mill, at the college lab or library or out with friends. It was too bad there wasn't more money around, Marcy thought, or she could campaign to go to that wilderness survival college camp that Cynthia Dankowitz had signed up for.

Now Janine was at the mill, taking an attitude as if she owned the place just because she'd lived in the neighborhood forever. It was too bad. At least Janine did things, unlike some of the other girls in class—Barbara and them—whose whole idea of conversation was who liked whom.

Marcy shrugged. She loved Charlie, and everybody knew it—even Charlie, she supposed. It wasn't the kind of thing where people ran around saying, "Marcy loves Charlie." She wouldn't have cared if they did. And Charlie? Well, if she knew Charlie, he'd just smile at her if they did that. He was so sweet. He was so—

He was here? Charlie Panucci was here at the mill, walking slowly down the driveway with a little girl by the hand. Katie Gooch. "Marcy?" he said, not surprised, as though he'd expected to find her here. "Is Eric here somewhere? He sent Katie for an umbrella."

"And for Julia," said Katie.

"Julia?" Marcy said.

"Why did he want Julia?" asked Charlie.

"Julia who?" asked Marcy.

"Julia Gagnon."

"Well, Janine is—" Marcy shaded her eyes as she walked up the steps and looked past the mill in the direction Janine had gone. Then she forgot Charlie, forgot Julia, forgot Katie, in her rush to find her aunt. "Kathleen!" she yelled as she burst in the mill door.

☺ J a n i n e

Mr. Lincoln swept into the Whole Learning classroom, grabbed the video camera out of Eric Gooch's hands, and plunked it down on his own desk. Then he turned furious eyes on Eric.

"This is the last straw, Gooch!" he shouted. "I don't know what they let you get away with in that fancy-pants school, but it's not going to happen in my classroom."

He hauled Eric out of his chair by his shirtfront, and

pushed his back up against the lockers. "Oof," Eric choked, the breath knocked out of him. "But my camera—" He reached toward Lincoln's desk.

"Just leave it lie," Mr. Lincoln growled. "You're coming with me." He shoved Eric toward the door. The Gooch winced; he was walking on his cast, without his crutches. I jumped up and handed him his crutches. He grabbed them, looking astonished, as though he expected Mr. Lincoln to take me in hand for helping him. Lincoln's head whirled toward me, his hair flying. "Sit down, Janine!" he said in a scary voice.

I would have given him my coldest scowl, right in the eye, but he had already turned and gone, manhandling Eric roughly out the door before him.

I was halfway back to my seat when Lincoln burst back in the door. "I'll be back in sixty seconds," he roared. "Not a move from any of you little twerps!"

The door slammed; the murmuring began.

"What do you think he *did*?" from Kelly Kim.

"What *could* he have done?" from Marcy Moreno.

"He must have videoed someone." That was Mike Marx.

"He videoed everyone!" Cynthia Dankowitz.

Suddenly I found myself leaping across the room toward Lincoln's desk. I snatched Eric's camera, dashed back to my desk, and dropped it into my backpack.

There was a great gasp from everyone in the room and then silence. Footsteps came down the hall, closer, and Mr. Lincoln entered the room.

I kept my eyes on Mr. Lincoln, but out of the corner of my eye I saw angry, scared faces.

"Pick up your pens," said Mr. Lincoln calmly. He was already passing out paper, business as usual—except what had he done with Eric Gooch? "You have five minutes to write down exactly what just happened, as you observed it."

"What?" Marcy Moreno's voice was loud. "You mean, you—"

"Not another word!" Lincoln said, sounding almost casual. The man truly had a screw loose. "And another thing. It's up to you to decide whether you'll identify the person who took the video camera from my desk. Of course I've observed that it's missing."

I ducked my head, letting my hair fall across my guilty face, and began writing in the back of the blue notebook I'd been using since my green one had gone missing a week ago.

My backpack was in the aisle, but I didn't dare reach out a foot to pull it closer. The evidence would have to stay where it was. Then again, other people had backpacks on the floor. Maybe I would slip out of this fix somehow.

Everyone around me was writing, quickly and furiously, as if the fate of Eric Gooch lay in his or her hands. I got busy, too, not wanting to incriminate myself.

"Mr. Lincoln?" Marcy's hand was in the air. "Should we write what we think about what we observed?" It was plain what Marcy thought, all right. I would have laughed if I'd dared.

The teacher gave her a stern look. "Just the facts, ma'am." He looked at his watch. "Four minutes." We wrote on.

"Time is *up*!" Mr. Lincoln announced. The classroom door opened, and Eric came in, all smiles. He smiled even wider when he saw that his camera was gone from Mr. Lincoln's desk. Then Mr. Lincoln walked over and shook Eric's hand, both of them wearing big, stupid grins.

"What's going on?" Clark Jamison burst out. And then suddenly everyone was talking, even louder and madder than before.

▶ *Eric*

Mr. Lincoln waved his hands and brayed, "Settle down!" They all got quiet fast. "You may have figured out that Mr. Gooch and I staged the event you just observed. It is, after all, still April—month of fools. Eric is to be commended for his acting talent." A murmur rose and fell. "I'm going to read each of your observations, without giving your name. There are several things I want you all to listen for. First, what did everyone observe? Second, what did only some observe? And third, what do people's observations show about their personal characteristics and convictions?"

He began to read someone's observation aloud:

We were all waiting for class to start when Mr. Lincoln entered the room. He pulled Eric Gooch out of his seat and started yelling at him. "You got away with this in your old school, but you're not going to get away with it here!" Eric looked shocked. Then Mr. Lincoln threw Eric up against the lockers and took his camera away. Then he took Eric out of the room. Janine brought him his crutches. And that was the last we saw of Eric.

It sounded like I was going to my doom.

He read another one:

At exactly 12:22 on April 30, the class was seated at their desks. Mr. Lincoln burst into the room and grabbed Eric Gooch. He yelled at him about something that happened at the Haycock School, and took his camera away and put it on his desk. Eric stood there terrified, leaning on the lockers. Mr. Lincoln started to take Eric out of the room, until Janine got him his crutches. Then he took Eric to the principal's office.

And from a critic:

Mr. Abe Lincoln finally had enough of Eric Gooch's snotty attitude and threw him out of class. He would have made Gooch hop all the way to the office, but Janine ran after him with his crutches.

It was astonishing. Every single person in that room had witnessed the exact same event, yet everyone recalled something completely different. Some acted offended (one of them was obviously Marcy). Others reported the news, as you'd expect Artie O'Halloran to (no emotion, but justice for all). Not a single one of them named the camera snatcher. I remembered something Mom said to Katie and me the other day when she came home to find all the English muffins eaten and nobody willing to own up. "You're not going to tell?" she'd said to us both, shaking her head, but with a smile in her eyes. "I guess there really is honor among thieves." She'd named us both guilty and sentenced us to clean up the kitchen.

⊘ *Janine*

Everybody else's observation stopped at the point when Mr. Lincoln and Eric Gooch left the room. Only mine went on: "On my way back to my seat I took Eric's video camera off Mr. Lincoln's desk and hid it in my backpack."

That was the end of my report. All through it I'd stared

straight ahead, my hands folded, hoping that nothing I'd said would betray my identity. Honest Abe would figure it out from the handwriting, I thought. But Eric wouldn't know. Well, there were still ten or so observations to read. I wouldn't get away with not naming myself. Somebody else was bound to.

But I was wrong. Of all those different observations, from all those many observers, not a single one named me, except for those who mentioned that I'd brought Eric's crutches to him.

By the time the last observation had been read, my heart was beating very loudly in my chest, and my palms were sweaty and cold. Why didn't they name me? It's not that I thought I would be in trouble—Mr. Lincoln treated the whole scene like it was a big game or some kind of comedy act—but that I couldn't believe my classmates would do this for me. Then I thought something I would have never thought a month ago, before I realized how much they didn't like me, before they all had turned against me for what I had said about Charlie Panucci.

It wasn't me they were out to help; it was Eric. He was a dweeb, and he used crutches, and he talked too much about the weather, but they *liked* him. They didn't think anyone should do anything to hurt him or blame him for anything he'd done. And they didn't think anyone, even me, should get in trouble for helping him.

"You all must have a very strong code of honor not to turn in your friend."

Their friend? Was that what I was? To them? To Eric?

Of the whole class, not a single person met my eyes. I bent over and opened my backpack, taking a deep breath while I was down there. Why was it so much harder to do something good than to do something bad? I forced myself to stand up, the video camera in my hand. I carried it over to Eric. He took it, his eyes on my face, but I couldn't look back at him. I went to my chair and sat down. I didn't know what to do with my hands or my eyes. The room was perfectly silent. I chanced a glance around at everyone, but still no one but Eric looked at me. I smiled from embarrassment, wishing I were invisible, completely invisible.

"I see." Mr. Lincoln finally spoke.

The bell rang, breaking the spell. Everyone stood up and began chattering, but no one said anything to me. I gathered my things and walked down the hall to the bus, and in my head I kept hearing Mr. Lincoln's last words. A stupid saying came into my head, something that Daddy says sometimes to tease me: " 'I see,' said the blind man, as he picked up his hammer and saw.' "

E R I C

SCIENCE OBSERVATION
APRIL 30

My reflections on our experiment:

How appalling to have Janine be the one to hand me my crutches—though, I reasoned, with our seats lined up alphabetically, and Gagnon coming before Gooch, she was closer to my crutches than Susan Hackman, who was next closest, almost as quick, and who would get my vote as Most Likely to Hand Me My Crutches.

Then to come back to the room and find my video camera gone! First, panic: Where was it? Was it in one piece? Still, I felt a little glow: Someone liked me enough to take back the camera they thought Mr. Lincoln had confiscated. *I* knew it was all a hoax, but nobody in the class did. Who was it? I got my hopes up again about Susan Hackman, but Cynthia Dankowitz sat closest to Mr. Lincoln's desk.

It was like getting a secret valentine (or how I imagine that to feel): Somebody cared, but I didn't know who, and the possibility in everybody's faces—jocks, dweebs, and everybody in between—made me realize that I would have been glad for any of them to have done it. It wasn't like Haycock. It could never be like Haycock. But if I had to stay here, I knew all at once, it would be okay.

But it became obvious that it was Janine who had taken the camera. I've been observing her so much that I couldn't stop now, and I don't know anyone else's face as well as hers. She must have turned about six different shades of pink, red, and white as she hid behind her hair and listened to the observations being read. Typical of her not to name herself when she admitted her guilt. But that was where the typical Janine ended and the surprise Janine emerged.

There she was, rising from where she'd been bent under her desk, walking bravely across the classroom, and handing me my camera, the one full of pictures of her looking really confused and left out and unlikable in dancing school last night.

And what about the rest of the class? *They* weren't surprised, were they? They'd seen her take the camera, after all. But not a single one of them told on her. Why not? Did she have, in truth, a single friend in the class? Or anywhere else?

Yes, I remembered: She had Katie. Katie had done nothing but blab on about Janine all week long. Janine took her to the pond to meet Kathleen. Janine told her about fish eggs and frog eggs. Janine was going to help her find some and keep them in a tank. Maybe they'd even grow legs! Janine said they'd find a way to keep Mini Pearl out of the way. And Katie didn't care what Julia or I said about Janine. She, Katie, was Janine's friend.

My dad once told me that in some countries if you save someone's life, he becomes your slave. Well, Janine didn't exactly save my life today, but when she thought I was in danger, she'd tried to save my camera. That didn't make me her slave, but it did make me feel I owed her something.

❏ *Eric*

I laid my observation notebook on the bookshelf next to my telescope. It was a good night to look at the stars: clear sky, no clouds. The earth had turned toward the sun and I could smell summer.

I hadn't let myself read Janine's notebook yet. I'd stuffed it into my dresser drawer the night I stole it from her kitchen, and it was still there. It shook me a little to open the drawer the next morning and find it there among my shirts. I hadn't read it then, either. Although I was a very observant person, I wasn't really nosy. Even with Mom at classes almost every afternoon, I never once read her journal or poked through her stuff. I'm not that kind of person. The next day, the day after Mr. Lincoln and I had staged our little play, I decided to make an exception.

All week long at school I had expected Janine to come flying out of nowhere, tackle me, pound me into the ground, and demand the return of her notebook. What had happened at school between Janine and me was a whole lot more unexpected. I nearly gave the green notebook back to Janine the next day, unread, once I realized what she had done. But something made me leave it home from school. Curiosity, I guess. And fear. If she found out *at school* that I had taken her notebook, what would she say? What might she do?

All that afternoon after school I thought about just walking across the street and putting the notebook in her mailbox or leaning it against the front door. But Julia was home, she and her boyfriend, and I was afraid they'd see me if I came sneaking around.

In science you are supposed to be able to make predictions. They are supposed to be based on what you know. Well, on the basis of what I knew about Janine, I would never have predicted that she'd be the one to save my video camera and me along with it.

Yes, I owed her something. I owed it to her to try to really understand her. It was my responsibility, I told myself, as her official observer.

I ignored what Mr. Lincoln had said about spying.

I stopped stewing about whether I was right or wrong, guilty or not guilty, and picked up her notebook.

Janine

I had been back to the mill several times, with and without Katie, taking the path from Kingfisher Lane down to the pond, searching the woods for my notebook. I still couldn't find it in the kitchen or my room or anywhere else when I looked for it after school. I wanted to take it along when I visited Kathleen. I had a feeling she would have interesting things to tell me, and I didn't want to forget a single one. And I thought that maybe it had fallen out of my backpack.

My stomach hurt, thinking about it: What if the fisherman had found it and read the stapled-down part about him? Would I ever get it back? Would I, could I dare to actually go up and ask him if he'd seen it? What if I had to go to Mr. Lincoln and tell him that I'd lost my whole term's observation?

I told myself that when I'd left last week, the fisherman had been on the other side of the pond. Kathleen had been walking all over the place, but she hadn't seen my notebook. Ten days of wandering around looking for notebooks and fish eggs. Sometimes Katie Gooch came along and looked with me. Once I saw Marcy Moreno sitting by the edge of the pond with a fishnet in her hand. She looked as dismayed as I felt. "Hi," I said.

She said hi back.

"What are you doing?" I asked.

"Collecting tadpoles," she said, as if it were something she did every day.

"Don't you have enough pets already?" I said, and moved on before she could answer.

But she yelled after me, "They're not for me!"

One day after school I decided to walk down Henry Street to get to the mill. The little mill driveway was muddy and shaggy along the edges. I liked the way it looked neglected, nothing like the perfect lawns on my street or the careful square gardens of Henry Street. I liked the muddy ruts made by the wheels of a truck of some kind.

The mill hung out over the pond, and the part that was on land faced onto this driveway. I'd never seen this side, though I was more than familiar with the pond side. Funny, it looked like a regular house with bushes and everything although it was plain from how worn out everything seemed that no one had lived here for years. An orange-striped cat appeared from the side of the house, and I bent low to have a conversation with him. We were just getting down to chin-scratching when a black Jeep crunched along the driveway, and Kathleen hopped out and started unloading groceries. She was in green and gray today, like a Girl Scout leader or a park ranger, like the colors of the pond under the gray sky. Was it camouflage?

Kathleen was a comfortable person who didn't ask questions, nice and friendly as long as you weren't squashing any fish eggs. She let me help her carry in her groceries. She didn't care if the cats walked all over the counter while we did it.

The first thing I did—made myself do—was ask her if she'd seen my notebook.

"Still haven't found it?" she asked, and looked up to see me shake my head. "Why don't you just get another one and start again?"

Well, that wasn't the point. I had, the day I'd met her. I

hadn't been able to find the green notebook, so I'd picked up a leftover math notebook from seventh grade and torn out the math pages at the beginning. That was my observation notebook now, and it seemed sort of appropriate since I wasn't observing myself anymore. Not officially, anyway.

"It's just. . . I have things in it. Observations."

"What sort of observations?" She was interested.

"For Whole Learning," I said. I kept my eyes on the whole-wheat bread and almond tea like Julia's and funny-looking, reddish orange lumps—pomegranates, she told me later.

"Oh, are you in that? So's my niece. Marcy Moreno. Lives right down the street."

I said, "Uh, Marcy?" and she said, "Yes." At the time I couldn't think of it as anything but bad news. After all, wasn't Marcy my enemy? She sure wasn't anything close to being my friend. But it was funny how often I thought of the baby guinea pigs, which must be all grown up by now. To have eighteen guinea pigs of your own; now that was something I liked to think about.

J A N I N E

[Written in the old blue notebook]
SCIENCE OBSERVATION
MAY 13

Kathleen Moreno is a biologist who's doing a study of our wetlands. Yesterday I had a lot of questions for her.

ME: "What are estuaries?" I've been reading up.

HER: "You don't know?"

ME: "No." What a dweeb, right? I didn't care if she knew I didn't know anything. Maybe that way she'd tell me more about the pond.

HER: "We're right *on* one, nearly. If you follow this river down just, oh, a mile or so, it starts to get brackish. Salty."

ME: "Because it gets near Long Island Sound?"

HER: "Right! And the animal life changes then. Different organisms. Different habitats. Different populations."

ME: "Different mud?" I wasn't being funny. I had really been wondering about that primordial ooze.

HER: "Oh, yes! Different mud!"

She showed me tadpoles she had growing in an aquarium. You could see the little knobs of legs coming out on some of them. She showed me fish eggs in cloudy balls, bigger ones. You could actually see how they might one day soon hatch into fish. She took me to the microscope in her kitchen, the room with all the windows that look out toward the cove, and showed me smaller eggs. She called them spawn. Then she showed me some slides with water on them.

HER: "This is the sound, a mile out. I went out in a friend's sailboat one day last week. And here's the mouth of your river—"

ME: "It's not *my* river."

HER: "It is if you want it to be."

I looked into her microscope.

ME: "It's dirty! It's full of *stuff.*"

HER: "Well, that's life."

Life is sure dirty. But she says worms and eggs and algae wouldn't do very well if the water was sterile.

I gazed at the things in the water: little eggs, cells of algae (she said), and ribbon-shaped worms. Two weeks ago I didn't know about any of this. I'd been outside those windows stomping the life out of fish eggs. Now I was inside seeing it all.

☺ *Janine*

The part I did not write down for Mr. Lincoln (I was still using my old blue math notebook) was the part about the fisherman.

"Come here," Kathleen said. She took me into a living room strewn with books and papers, cameras, and other hard-at-work kinds of stuff. She walked over to the window and pointed out.

"There!" she said. "That's proof for you!"

I looked and jumped in shock. This window looked out at the river end of the millpond. There stood the fisherman, his pretty hair not looking very shiny today in the cloudiness. "When you see that," said Kathleen, "it's always a good sign."

I forced myself to speak. "How long have you been staying here?" My stomach was shivering. What had she seen? Had she seen the fisherman *close up*?

"Day before last," she said. "It took me a while to get

moved in. I had so much equipment to move." She was peering through some binoculars. "Look there! I believe he's caught a bass!"

I touched her sleeve. "Show me something else in the microscope," I said.

❥ *Eric*

I'd been sitting thinking for what seemed like hours, holding Janine's green book in my lap, when Janine herself knocked on the door. I hid the notebook under my math book and went to the door.

Janine's face was glowing. I don't think I've ever seen her look so happy. "Katie here?" she said without even saying hello. "There's something I want to tell her."

"Katie had a play date today. She'll be home by five-thirty." I could tell by the light in the trees that it was almost five o'clock now.

"Oh," Janine said. "Well, tell her I have some frog eggs to show her."

"Why? What have *you* been doing?"

"They were at the pond," she said.

After reading what I'd read this afternoon, I didn't want to think she'd ever go to the pond again. And I certainly didn't want Katie to go there.

"Are the eggs at your house?"

"No," she said. "Down there. That woman, Kathleen? She's letting me hatch them."

"Good!" I said, and tried to sound enthusiastic. But it was

all too strange, Janine in my doorway smiling, while behind me in the living room . . .

I hopped across the hall through the living room and picked up her notebook. With my back to her, I heard her say, close behind me, "Listen, Gooch? About that time when Katie was home alone because you went to see Charlie? I just wanted to say"—I blocked the book with my body—"whenever you want to go see Charlie, you can leave Katie with me."

"Why would I do a thing like that?" I thought it must have been the first time in her life that she'd ever offered to do anything nice for anyone.

"No reason," she snapped.

"What's come over you lately?" I said. "You're like a saint or something." She just walked toward the door. She didn't want to hear it and was probably already sorry that she'd made the offer. I sat down, right on the notebook, and I called after her, "It was nice of you to try to save me from Mr. Lincoln." She shook her head, made a throwing-me-away gesture with her hand, and opened the door. "Janine, wait!" I managed to choke out.

She came back into the room and stood with one tentative hand on the piano. "Yeah?" she said in her tough voice. This wasn't going to be easy.

"I have to tell you something," I said. She watched me with her dark eyebrows drawn together. I went on, practically babbling. "I was mad at you about what you said about Charlie, and I was upset that I forgot Katie, and somehow I thought it was part of my science project, and the opportunity arose to get a look at—" I pulled the notebook out from beneath me.

She gasped. Her eyes got white around the edges, and she grabbed the book from my hand and spun into the foyer. I hopped up and went after her as quickly as I could. She was already out the front door. "Janine, I'm sorry!" I said. Her back in her yellow T-shirt was as unforgiving as it had ever been; she didn't slow a bit. But I was in it now. No turning back.

"Janine!" The catch in my hollering voice sent Mini Pearl running out the door almost as fast as Janine. "You should tell someone, Janine! About that *fisherman*!" She was going, scurrying across the street to the safe sanity of her house. "Tell *somebody*!" Her door slammed. She was gone.

Chapter 9

Julia runs so hard her heart hurts. It has been a long time since she's been to the wetlands, but she remembers every inch of the path, every root that might trip her, every stone. She used to come down here a long time ago, to climb a tree and write her diary and her stories. It has always felt like a place outside the world, a safe place that never changes. Whatever she was pouring out onto paper, being there among the trees, near the water, smelling the marsh, always made her calm. Her feelings and ideas never made any difference to the bluff and the pond and the rocks. Beside them, her feelings were small, and being small was safe.

Small like Janine is. Safe like Janine is not.

She reaches the hill that ends in the big bluff above the pond. Jeff is there at the bottom, right where he said he'd meet her. He is unbuckling the Rollerblades that got him here so fast. In the sandy soil of the wetlands he wouldn't get far on skates. Eric Gooch is sitting in the grass above him, at the top of the bluff, just where Katie said he would be. Julia begins to climb toward him.

Jeff has one skate off and is taking off the other one when he feels the rain begin. He looks up at the sky, hears thunder in the distance, and considers running up the hill after Julia, in his sweat socks. Instead, he pulls the skate back on and heads back toward the road.

Jeff has never skated so fast up Kingfisher Lane. He goes right into the kitchen on his skates and picks up the phone. He dials the number for his father's beeper, leaves him a message to come home fast. He calls the police, then he dodges outside, where the rain is growing steadier. There in the road stands Mrs. Gooch. He's a few strides away when a sound in the distance brings him to a halt. He can see in Mrs. Gooch's face that she hears the sirens, too. She steps toward him.

"Do you know where Eric and Katie are?"

◗ *E r i c*

After school the next day I came straight home, made Katie a peanut butter and bologna sandwich, her favorite, and hugged her for courage. Then I called the Gagnons' house. If Janine answered, I intended to hang up the phone. I had my finger on the button when I heard Julia's voice. "Is Janine there?" I said in my formal voice.

"No, I'm sorry," said Julia. "May I take a message?"

"It's me, Eric Gooch. Where did she go?"

"Out for a walk," she said.

"Where?" I felt panicked. "To the wetlands?"

"I don't think so. She went the other way."

I took a breath. "Listen, I have to talk to you right now. Can I come over?"

When I walked into their kitchen, I saw that Jeff was there with Julia. Okay, I told myself. I tried to breathe deeply as I got Katie parked in front of the Gagnons' television, something she rarely gets to do on a school day. Jeff was Janine's brother, and it might be easier to say what I had to say with a guy there.

It wasn't.

For one thing, Jeff didn't speak a word of encouragement the whole time I spoke. He sat on a stool and ate a bowl of Cheerios and mostly looked at the Cheerios.

Julia was the one who made me a cup of almond tea, then looked at my face intently as I told about the fisherman in the wetlands.

"What you're saying, Eric, is that Janine made friends with a fisherman?"

"Well, I don't think they're friends, exactly, but they've spoken to each other. They say hi. But then this one time—Janine was up on the hill, and she looked down and saw him by the pond. She didn't think he knew she was there, and at first he didn't, but then he realized. And he—I'm not sure, but I think, no, I really am very sure—"

"What, for Pete's sake?" This from Jeff.

"He was—"

"*What?*" from Julia.

"It wasn't—"

"Just say it, please; it concerns my sister." That was Julia.

"Playing with himself."

Jeff's voice was terrible and quiet. "You mean, jerking off?"

"Masturbating," whispered Julia. From the next room the television blared Elmer Fudd. Our heads were down, our faces purple. Then Julia leaped to her feet.

"Did he touch her?" She was furious now, as was Jeff, silent, waiting.

I shook my head, hard.

"Did he go *near* her?" Frightened, too.

"No. He just turned around in her direction. He let her know he knew she was there."

Jeff laughed and went on too long, like a hyena. "A flasher!" he howled. "Janny met a real live flasher!"

Julia glared at him. "Shut up, Jeff," she said.

"Aw, come on." Her brother waved his hands casually. "It's not like anything actually happened."

His words hung in the air, and I suddenly felt unsure.

"You don't think anything happened?" Julia's eyes were pale. "Picture the scene. No, he didn't touch her. No, he didn't talk to her. He just stood there and smiled and—"

She laid her forehead on the table and wrapped her arms around her head. She sat and shuddered, embarrassed to death and angry and scared. I reached out and touched her arm. I'd never touched her at all before. She didn't even seem to notice. I raised my hand to her shoulder and patted her a little. I glanced at Jeff, who was dark red, still giggling into his cereal bowl.

"Julia?" I said at last. "I know I shouldn't suggest this, and you know what *she'd* say—" I paused, then burst out, "I can get him on video, Julia."

"*What?*" Jeff yelped.

We all stared at one another, equals. It was a moment worth recording except that I felt so completely sick to my stomach.

✆ *Janine*

The next afternoon as soon as I got home, I went back to Kathleen's house. I went the Henry Street way, to make sure Eric wouldn't see me.

As I walked, I saw a big van pull up in the Panuccis' driveway. All the little Panuccis came piling out, and then came Charlie. I kept on walking and glancing back, trying not to look like I was looking. I saw Charlie climb out and begin to walk, very slowly and stiffly, up the sidewalk to his house.

I didn't think Charlie saw me. I wanted to run back and say something, but what would I say? Not a single word came to me, and after standing there stupidly on the sidewalk for a minute, I kept going and turned into the dirt driveway to the mill.

The black Jeep was gone. Both cats, the orange tabby and the white one, were sitting on the stone steps, so I sat there with them and had a talk. I hoped she would come back soon, I told the cats, because I had something important to tell her. I stared at the tire ruts in the driveway and thought about the fisherman.

Somehow being here, by the mill, and thinking about telling Kathleen the whole thing made it all very real all over again, and sitting there, I started to shiver. *Stop it*, I told myself. *Calm down*. What was the gigantic big deal, anyway? He hadn't exactly been trying to catch me and murder me. But my mind argued back: Maybe he shouldn't have been letting anyone see.

That's when I jumped to my feet and headed down the steps toward the pond. I would go and find him and look him in the eye and tell him to stay away from me, to do his private stuff at home in the bathroom like a normal human. If there's one thing I can do, it's make people do what I say.

But when I got to the pond, the fisherman was not there, and suddenly I felt weak and tired and foolish. So I had seen his penis (there, I made myself say it). So what? I had just happened to see him using the pond for a toilet. It was just rudeness, like picking your nose when you don't think anyone can see. And it was just my bad luck to happen to see him. Nothing had happened to *me*.

I stopped thinking about it.

I forced myself to think of Charlie Panucci instead. All the girls said he was so sweet. Well, he never was sweet to me. Why was that? He had soft-looking, curly dark hair. I walked slowly along the shore of the pond, and I couldn't stop thinking of what Charlie must look like now and how he was feeling. It didn't matter what I felt, I told myself; Charlie was the one who was hurt.

I was worried for Kathleen. What if she had gone out exploring alone, and he— I was worried about Katie, too. That was why I had gone to the Gooches', to offer to look out for her. She had come to the wetlands once, looking for me. What was to stop her from doing it again, when her mother was out working, her father was gone, and Eric was visiting Charlie Panucci?

The afternoon I got my notebook back, what with Eric yelling about what was in it, I never got to say what I wanted to about Charlie Panucci: that I hoped he was going to be okay. I never got to warn Kathleen, either. I sat on her step until my bottom was cold and sore, and then I figured she was gone for the day. I stood up and went home.

SCIENCE OBSERVATION
MAY 18

Charlie Panucci has been thinking about Janine, too.

"I hear you have a rescuer," he said to me.

Now who did he hear that from? "Marcy told me," Charlie said. "She described the whole dramatic scene. They all thought Lincoln was going to drink your blood. And there was Janine, like Mighty Mouse. 'Here I come to save the day!' " He sang the words, then subsided a little. Looked like it hurt him to talk loud or sing, but he kept forgetting it. I guess that is a good sign.

"Some mouse," I said.

"She might be turning over a new leaf," said Charlie.

I snorted. "Don't hold your breath." Secretly I think she is trying. But the last thing I need—after Janine's big rescue scene—is for anyone to think I'm having soft thoughts toward her. Even Charlie.

But if there's one thing I've learned from studying people, it's that they're surprising, like spring squalls.

Charlie said, "She sent me a get-well card."

I could have fainted from shock, but I hid it well. "So? After all these years of torment, you're going to let her off the hook because of one stupid get-well card?"

"It felt like an apology."

"For what? Your whole life?" I knew for what: for that

145

comment she'd made that was all over school from the moment she said it. But did Charlie know about it? Is that what he meant? Who would have told him?

Charlie just looked at me. I could see he wondered what *I* had against Janine. What had she ever done to me, he must have wondered, other than make a few obnoxious comments at the bus stop?

He said, "I could have killed myself with that hot water, Eric. Maybe she's glad I didn't."

I just nodded, thinking Charlie didn't like it that I was being mean about Janine. Charlie went on. "*I'm* glad I didn't. And if somebody else agrees, then who am I to argue?"

If there is one thing I've learned from observing Janine Gagnon all spring long, from far away, from close up, in school and out of school, it is that she needs a little help. And if anyone else turned around and started acting as if Janine Gagnon were a human being, it might not make as much of a difference to her as it would if Charlie did it. He was a star now, scar and all.

"I think she's not so bad," I said.

Charlie shrugged. Then he seemed to remember: Shrugging hurt.

"Smart, too."

He nodded.

I gave it my final shot. "And pretty," I said. He rolled his eyes. "She has eyes the color of root beer."

"Oh, really? Just your type?"

"Susan Hackman is my type," I said.

"Come on, surprise me," said Charlie.

"I mean it," I said. I stood next to the television and pointed out the girls in dancing school. "You could have any girl in the eighth grade, you know."

"Get out of the way, Gooch," Charlie said. He pretended to fast-forward me with the remote control.

"So which one will you have?" I asked. "Kelly Kim, I bet that's who."

"Oh, Mom," called Charlie, sounding like one of his little sisters, "Gooch is bothering me!"

"I know who likes you," I said, but there was something in me that didn't want to tell tales on Marcy. He'll figure it out for himself soon enough. At least we were off the subject of Janine.

☺ *Janine*

My sister, Julia, really went too far one night. I finally got a chance to tell her about Kathleen Moreno and the frogs' eggs, and I don't think she paid attention to a word I said. She was fidgety and nervous as if—I don't know, as if she had found out Lionel had seen her in her underwear or something.

I asked her as much. "My underwear?" she said, as if I'd said a swearword. "Whatever makes you say that?"

When my story wound down, she never even mentioned it—not a word of response about Kathleen or eggs or the millpond. "Janine," she said, "have you ever"—she blushed and twisted her class ring and said, looking quickly up at me—"touched yourself?"

I stared at her. She blushed darker, drew herself up, then collapsed onto the bed, sighing. What was wrong with her?

"Sure," I said. "I've touched myself a lot. I touch myself all the time." I put out one hand and touched the other with it. "See? Touch! Oops, excuse me, self, did I touch you?"

"Jan*ine*," she said, getting all stuffy, "I mean, *sexually*."

Sexually?

She had that "Boy, you're dumber than I thought" look on her face—surprise and sympathy and dismay—so I said, "I *know* about sex, Julia. And I also know that it takes two people. *Two*, Julia. A person cannot have sex all alone."

She closed her eyes and looked like she felt sick. "A person can pretend," she said quietly.

Pretend?

My eyes were as wide open as hers were tightly shut. I couldn't understand the whole idea of sex in the first place. I mean, I knew what happened technically, but the reasons behind it escaped me. I guessed I really must be—what Julia and Mother had said—immature for my age.

With her eyes locked shut against me, Julia made a little blind speech. "There are feelings that people try to re-create, invent, on their own. In privacy. That's why you don't know about it, Jan, because people don't talk about it."

"*You* are."

"This is private, Janine. You and me, we're private. And so should sex be private—*any* kind, alone or together."

"Well, you don't have to be so worried about *me*," I cried out. "I'm not having sex with anyone. Are you, Julia?"

She lay back on the bed and stared at the ceiling. "There's a man in the wetlands, Janine. I think he goes fishing there?"

"You've seen him?" I leaned forward. "With the shiny brown hair?"

She leaned up on one elbow and stared at me. "I haven't ever seen him," she said, "but you've seen a lot of him, haven't you?"

It was the way she said it, not that I'd seen him often, but that I'd seen more of him than just shiny brown hair.

"Well, once I caught him going to the bathroom. At least I thought he was going to the bathroom," I told her. I dropped my voice to a whisper, worried suddenly that Jeff might overhear us. "Nothing, really. He was peeing, that's all."

"I don't think so," said Julia. "Eric told me what you saw."

"Eric Gooch!" I cried. I'd kill him. Jeff could hear me loud and clear if he were listening. "He can't even walk into the wetlands! Well, maybe he couldn't a month ago, but now that the snow's gone and the mud is dry—"

"Janine! He read your notebook. He read about what you were looking at. He's seen the guy. And he put two and two together. That man shouldn't have been there, Jan. He shouldn't have been doing what he was doing. And he shouldn't have let you see."

"How do *you* know?"

She was staring at me, and I was staring at her, and one of us was about to cry, and it wasn't me, no, sir. Whatever she saw in my face sent her over the edge, and sniffling, she said, "Eric's going to get him on video, Janny. You and I are going to help him. And then we're going to call the cops."

"The cops?"

"He shouldn't be doing this, Janine. It's against the law."

If the cops knew, then everyone I knew would find out. When I opened my mouth to say so, nothing came out but tears. Julia held me as if I were Katie, patting my head and stroking my hair and crooning over and over, "It's okay, it's okay."

◗ *Eric*

I went to the doctor and got my hard hip cast removed and a new softer one put on that actually allowed me to move my knee, which wasn't easy. I still had crutches, but pretty soon, the doctor said, I could start to walk with a cane.

I was walking up and down Kingfisher Lane practicing, with Katie zipping around on her bike, when Jeff Gagnon came out. He sat down on his front steps and pulled on his Rollerblades. I expected him to take off, but instead, he came skating over to where I was.

"We've been making a plan," he said.

"You and Julia?" I said, sounding like a dope.

"Julia is following Janine's schedule closely." It was like a James Bond movie. "We're going to try to set that guy up."

"How?" I stared at my feet, not wanting to ask the question that was growing inside me day after day. "Shouldn't we tell your parents?"

Jeff sighed. "We've been arguing about that, but listen, this is what we really think: If we do, they'll go to the police. But there won't be any evidence. Just her word against his, and she's a kid."

"So?"

Katie rode past and knocked my Red Sox hat off my head. I swatted her bottom before she got away. Jeff did a slow spin on his skates and turned back to me.

"He'll say he was taking a piss in the pond, and how will anyone know he wasn't?"

We were both silent, looking at our feet. My foot felt funny, cool in the air, without all that hard fiberglass pressing on it.

"We've got to catch him at it," Jeff went on. "Someday when it's not a great hiking day so people won't be there walking around. In the rain, maybe, when it's good fishing weather."

"That won't be great for filming, though."

"Oh." He looked concerned, as if he thought I was an expert.

"Well, if she's by the pond, there'll be reflected light. Maybe Janine should pretend to be fishing."

"Yeah," said Jeff. Then the color changed again in his face, as if suddenly it made him nervous just thinking about it. "He's a molester," he said quietly. "He'll hurt her if he gets near her."

Katie knocked my hat off again. "Why should he?" I said. "He didn't get anywhere near her before. Why should he this time? We'll set it up like it was before, so he thinks she's looking. Only we'll really be setting him up."

"And then?"

"Get it on video," I said, low and strong. "Take the video to the police. He'll be all unsuspecting. He'll show up at the pond, and that'll be it."

We figured out the angles and made a plan. I'd be up on the bluff, where I could see the whole pond but not be seen. Julia would take the driveway from Henry Street, and Jeff would cover the Kingfisher Lane entrance. That way, he reasoned, if the fisherman took off, Jeff could give chase on his Rollerblades, and even hang on to the back of the creep's van if he had to. The guy couldn't go very fast down Kingfisher Lane.

It was as good as done. "One thing," said Jeff. "Somebody ought to be assigned to get his license plate number. If we had any brains, we would have done that before."

"Someone will." I shrugged. I was starting to feel sick with nervousness myself.

"Katie," suggested Jeff. "She can write, can't she? We can station her on Kingfisher Lane, on her bike."

My heart stopped. "Katie stays out of this," I said. "I don't want this to have anything to do with my sister."

Jeff watched my eyes. "Well, both my sisters are involved," he said.

"But they're older! They're big."

We both thought of Janine. "Janine is still such a shrimp," Jeff said. "I keep wondering when she's going to get taller. Anyway, she'll save the whole neighborhood from perverts."

"One pervert," I said.

"Are there others?" Jeff laughed in an embarrassed way.

I looked at him. He was joking, nervous. Well, I was nervous, too. I sighed. "Tell Julia I'm ready. Tell her to say when."

Chapter 10

*J*ulia is halfway up the bluff when she hears Janine's voice. She stands still, dumbfounded at her sister's courage and, she admits it, frightened by the anger and pain in her voice. If it were she, Julia, she'd be running. She would have run the first time, that time Janine wrote about in the notebook, and would have never come back alone. Yes, that would have been the sensible thing for Janine to do, just stay away, just avoid the wetlands altogether. But Janine has never had that much sense. How sensible is it to make enemies of the whole neighborhood? How sensible is it always to try to beat all of them—boys and girls—at whatever they're best at?

Not that she, Julia, had all that much sense. She was supposed to be the older one, the mature one, the one getting ready to go to college. Oh, why didn't she go along with her instinct to tell her parents, tell that wetlands woman, tell the cops about what was happening to Janine?

Because she wasn't sure. The boys were so—what was the best word?—hyped on the subject. Eric had read this passage in Janine's journal and decided a whole, big perverted event had taken place at the pond. He and Jeff had come up with this plot to catch the fisherman before Julia even knew what was happening.

She went along because she thought there was time, that Janine really wasn't going to come down here again, that the boys weren't going to do anything silly with that video camera. But there was another reason she waited. She knew what the police might say if she told them, how they might be skeptical. Really, it was all so—word?—cloudy, confused, inexact. Weren't boys always doing things like mooning cars out the back of the lacrosse team bus? Lionel had told her about being in gym class with girls; while he'd been standing there talking to a girl he liked, his friend—his friend!—had come up and pulled down his shorts. Was this different? Yes. No. How?

Too late for all that, Julia, she tells herself. Things have been taken out of her slow-moving, inept hands and placed in—oh, God!—Janine's.

And now Julia is amazed by the words that are coming out of Janine's mouth. Well, Janine has always had a big mouth, Julia knows that, but she didn't know she knew so many swearwords. It's defense, she realizes suddenly. Janine has her claws out. In defense of her little sister, Julia's claws emerge, too, and she sprints to the top of the bluff.

☙ Janine

Promise or no promise, I had to go to the wetlands and look for the fisherman. Somehow I had to solve this myself, let him know he was in trouble with me and everyone else, get him to leave me alone, and, if I could, get him to go away altogether. The night before, as I was nearly asleep and walking around the pond in my mind, I'd suddenly thought of Marcy, sitting there with her fishnet, scooping out tadpoles. I hadn't ever bumped into her before, so I thought maybe she'd just started coming after Kathleen arrived. Who else had she bumped into besides me?

Kathleen was right: It *was* my pond, my river, as much as I wanted it to be. Or it had been until *he* had shown up. But there was another reason I wanted to be at the pond: Kathleen herself and the fish. I had so many questions to ask. I couldn't stay away.

Something new had a hold on me. I couldn't stop wondering whether the little fish had hatched yet. And why did they even need to hatch, in the larger scheme of things? Fishwise, didn't they do just as much good floating around as eggs as they would swimming around as fish? I wanted to ask Kathleen that, that and a hundred other things. I also wanted to see for myself. But I had promised Julia, promised Jeff, even promised Eric that I wouldn't go to the pond on my own.

So I didn't. It's true, all week long I really didn't. On Tuesday I managed to get behind Marcy and Cynthia in the lunch line. "Find any tadpoles lately?" I asked casually.

"Plenty," said Marcy simply, while Cynthia's face showed as much emotion as the cement-block wall behind her. All kinds of things went through my head to say: Stay close to your aunt. Don't go there alone. Watch out for a man with a fishing pole. Instead, I leaned toward her and said in a dark voice, "You never know where you'll run into weirdos."

"Who, like you?" Cynthia rolled her eyes and turned away, but Marcy just gave me a shrug.

"Who's the little girl you took to see Kathleen?" she asked.

"Eric Gooch's sister," I answered. She smiled and followed Cynthia into the cafeteria with her tray.

I waited until Friday to go to the wetlands again. After school I walked along Henry Street, taking the muddy driveway to the millhouse. Kathleen's house. Mr. Lincoln had written a note in my blue notebook to tell me that it wasn't too late to change my observation subject. The green notebook was buried in the back of my bedroom closet.

I loved the idea that Kathleen was here, completely independent—no family except a brother up the street, no husband, just cats and frogs and little fishes—just working and watching and waiting to see how things would develop.

There was something else I loved about Kathleen. I thought of it as I sat down in her kitchen—she was home!—and watched her put the kettle on. It was this: She smiled at me in a way no other adult ever had. She didn't know anything about me, that's why, had never heard me say anything snide or sneering about anyone, had never had her feelings hurt by me, had so far never been surprised by anything I said. All Kathleen knew was that I was here in her kitchen on a gray afternoon, that I liked her, that I loved the pond the way she did, that I was hungry to learn all I could about it.

I crossed my arms and hugged myself, wishing somehow that I could keep this happy feeling, stay in this safe place, stay new and positive and unknown. If only this day would get better, instead of worse. If only I didn't have to tell Kathleen to watch out for a guy who might start pretending something right in front of her.

Then there was a knock on the door, and Marcy Moreno came in, without even waiting for Kathleen to open the door.

She zoomed right over to the fish tank, bent down, and peered at the tadpoles. "Kathleen!" she called out. "Jumping Jacqueline has legs!" Kathleen came into the room then, with the teapot in her hand, and Marcy turned and saw me sitting there.

"Janine!" she said, and that was the only word, but there was so much in it of dismay, if not plain dislike, that my eyes flew to Kathleen's face, sure I would read some awful change there. Well, I knew it had to happen sometime.

But Kathleen's smile didn't change at all. She just said, "Well, of course you two know each other!" and she whisked back into the kitchen and returned with a teacup for Marcy.

"Hi," I managed to choke out. But Marcy was on the other side of the room by then, busily checking out all the wildlife and seeing what was new since her last visit, which seemed to have been only yesterday. She didn't pay any attention to me. Kathleen came back with the tea, and Marcy came and sat beside her. To make conversation, I asked Kathleen why the fish needed to hatch out of the eggs at all.

She was stumped at first. "That's a question in the spirit of Darwin," she said. I didn't know what that meant. I waited for the answer. "It's the way of the world," she went on. "Things just *have* to grow, don't they?"

"But why?" said Marcy. "In terms of evolution? Why couldn't they stay eggs and be food for other things, since that's what most of them turn into, anyway?" I was surprised. That was *just* what I'd meant by my question.

Hearing Marcy, I realized I knew the answer. "Because there wouldn't be enough food in the eggs for them," I said, feeling smart. "There must be just enough to make them grow as big as the egg, and then they're too big, plus there isn't any more food."

"I think so," said Kathleen slowly, thinking about it.

"Do they hatch so they can find their own food?" suggested Marcy.

"Either that, or they get eaten themselves," I said, and Marcy looked to see if I was being, well, being my usual self. But I hadn't meant anything by the comment.

Then Kathleen said, "Janine, would you like to have your own egg collection to study, like Marcy's?"

So those were Marcy's tadpoles, huh? Who did she think she was? I felt lonely, knowing that Marcy was established here before me. She was related and everything. But Kathleen was asking me to join in and be part of things.

I dared to look at Marcy to see how she was taking it and saw the same confusion in her pond brown eyes behind her glasses as must have shown in my own. Kathleen looked from one of us to the other and said, "Marcy, why don't you take Janine and show her where the best spawning places are?"

We went down the cellar steps and gathered buckets, then took off our shoes and waded into the little cove of the millpond.

▶ *Eric*

I walked to the wetlands with Katie on Friday afternoon, doing a test run to see if my leg in its new cast could deal with the damp, grassy ground and the sand. I was nervous, plotting my video, thinking of what I might have to do, what I might see, how I might have to sneak around.

It occurred to me that I was getting this too built up in my head. I had been thinking a lot about Janine's fisherman. "Flasher," Jeff had called him. Now what would anyone need to flash for? *That* was abnormal. Where did *that* come from?

Kids were weird, and mean, and even cruel sometimes, but they had nothing on adults for messing up people's lives.

Just last night my mother had told me, "Your father's going to talk to you about Haycock. He wants you to go back." I'd stood up from the dinner table without a word and gone upstairs to the weather station. I sat on the roof and looked at the evening sky, still light at eight o'clock. I checked over my feelings as though I were looking for my pulse. Angry? Sad? Resentful? Which one of them would make any difference to my father?

When it came to the case of the fisherman flasher, I was the person who would change the way things went. I could make him stop. I would catch him on camera—flash!—and he would be history. And Janine—and Julia and Katie and the rest of the girls in the neighborhood—would be safe. Well, if there's one thing I've learned from studying meteorology, it's just how wrong I can be. When it came to the crucial point, I wasn't going to be the hero at all.

Now Katie and I were trudging around the pond, on safari. That's what she thought it was, anyway. We'd come here right after school. Katie had her red rubber boots on her feet and her lunch box in her hand. My binoculars and my video camera hung around my neck. I had a huge, heavy stick that I was using to haul myself up the back of the bluff.

"Be vewy quiet! We're hunting wabbits!" I hushed Katie in my best Elmer Fudd voice, wanting to give her the idea of prowling around silently. We went along without talking until we reached a lookout place on the hilltop with a few rocks that hid us from view.

"Are those the wabbits?" Katie pointed down at the pond, and there was Janine. She was wading in the pond—why now? Why today?—and Marcy Moreno was with her.

I was annoyed. Janine had *promised* she wouldn't come to

the wetlands again, yet there she was. She hadn't used our road and the back path. She'd taken Henry Street, I supposed, and gone down the road that comes out across the pond by the deserted mill. But what was Marcy Moreno doing with her? And why were they dabbling there in the water, so close to the old mill building? This was strange.

"Dastardly intwuders!" I said to Katie, still being Elmer. "We mustn't be spotted!" Katie and I crouched behind the rocks, giggling. Well, it was as good a trial run as any. If Marcy and Janine didn't hear us or see us, nobody else would.

⚇ *Janine*

"Careful!" I said. "There are ten million tiny fish eggs in here."

Marcy almost laughed, then turned to look into my face. She was quite tall, so it wasn't surprising that so few boys ever wanted to dance with her at dancing school.

"Why are you being so nice lately?" she demanded.

I gulped, because right then of course I wasn't being nice on the inside. And, anyway, I hadn't meant to be nice on the outside. It's just that I had been thinking of something else: When was I going to get a chance to talk to Kathleen alone? Now there was Marcy to worry about, too. This whole thing was getting out of hand. The wetlands used to be my place, my place alone. Now that it was getting dangerous, it was getting busy, too.

"I—I like it here," I managed to say.

She nodded. "Yeah, me, too. My mother found this place."

"Found it? It's been here for two hundred years!"

"Found it for Kathleen, I mean. We knew she was looking for a research situation, and my mother brought her over from Storrs to show her this."

"Oh. I—"

She was bending over, looking into the water, dipping her net in. "What?"

I shook my head, but Marcy didn't see. She scooped up a glob of jelly with little eggs inside and laid it gently in the pond water inside the bucket. Then she looked up at me.

"Did you hear about Charlie?" Her voice was low, and oh, no, I thought, don't tell me he's back in the hospital, or sicker, or dead. "He's coming back to school!" She sounded full of happiness.

I'm not dumb, and Marcy's face was an open book.

"Marcy," I said slowly, "who did you choose to observe all this term?"

She stiffened and said nothing but didn't act embarrassed the way some people would have. She stood there peering into the green water with the net poised above it.

"Was it Charlie?" I asked.

She looked at me hard then and could only say, "Yeah, but—"

"And who was Charlie observing?"

"Can't you guess?"

I pictured Charlie. I saw him on the bus, leaning forward from the seat he shared with Eric Gooch to talk to Marcy. I saw Eric Gooch sitting next to him in the cafeteria. I saw Charlie and Jeff skating around Eric in the middle of Kingfisher Lane.

"Gooch?" I hooted. "Where's the interest there?"

Marcy whirled on me then, and her net dripped all over

her rolled-up jeans. "Where's the interest in hating every-one?"

I took a step back, her anger was so quiet and strong, and nearly slipped. "But I don't," I said. It was true.

Marcy's face changed. She wasn't sure she believed me, I could see that. She said, "At first Charlie was interested in the broken leg. He's always trying to understand how things work, how they go together. But then he got to like Eric, so it was easy."

I wondered how Eric would respond if he heard that Charlie was friends only for the sake of science. Marcy went on. "Well? What about you? Who were you observing?"

I couldn't say "myself." It had started to seem kind of con-ceited. I admitted only, "I've changed my observation. I'm going to do Kathleen now."

"Oh, that's a *good* idea!" Marcy's enthusiasm gave me a warm feeling in my chest. Maybe Marcy was just acting friendly for Kathleen's sake, but I didn't really think so. I thought it was just how Marcy was. It was a pretty interesting way to be.

◗ *Eric*

I settled my back against a rock, wondering if it was too early in the season for deer ticks to be lurking in the tall weeds. I turned on my camera and took a few views of the sky. Gray clouds were coming in from the west. Rain was on its way, and plenty of it.

I put down my camera to study the clouds, and that's when

I saw it. The white van was pulling up near the entrance at the end of our road. I could just see it among the trees.

"Lie down, Kate!" I urged. "What do you see in those clouds?" I pulled her head into the crook of my arm and cuddled her, and we lay there among the grass, looking at the sky. My leg throbbed wickedly from changing position so fast.

I lay there—invisibly, I hoped—as long as I could, until I was sure the fisherman had had time to gather his tackle and make his way to the pond.

At last I sat up and looked around the rock. Good Lord, he was right there, just twenty feet below us, messing around with his buckets and rods. I felt a raindrop on my nose.

"Kate?" I said. "I'm sending you on an important mission."

"Where?" She imitated my low voice.

"To Master Spy Julia," I said. "Tell her that we require an umbrella. Ask her to bring it herself!"

"Are you staying here?"

"Yes," I said. "My leg—it's busted, boss. I may not make it to morning."

She giggled. "Oh," she said.

"Hurry, Katie," I said. "And watch the road." Katie scurried off down the hill, making a shower of little rocks, but the fisherman, still banging his buckets around, seemed not to hear.

But then I saw that Janine had seen him, too. I watched as she said something to Marcy and then walked away from her, around the far side of the pond. She walked very slowly, tapping her little aquarium net against her thigh.

Chapter 11

*I*t becomes obvious that Janine's feet are rooted to the ground, are in fact sending down shoots to keep her from moving without a major gust of wind or some other act of God. Marcy, she thinks. Marcy was beside her just a moment ago. They were wading in the marsh together, looking for fish eggs. It was so nice. Marcy was calm, and kind, and even friendly.

Maybe Marcy is still there, in the marsh. Maybe she'll look across the pond and see Janine frozen there, too close to the fisherman, dangerously close, in fact. Marcy will do something. Marcy will save her.

Janine's eyes sweep the marsh area, seeking out Marcy. Big surprise: Marcy is gone. Who can blame her? What has Janine ever done for Marcy, after all?

She is on her own, under the stormy sky, that frightening man in front of her. She focuses her eyes on his face, only on his face and never downward, and feels big, square words begin to form.

▶ *Eric*

Janine made her way, head down, along the rocks of the far shore. You're breaking your promise, I said to her in my mind, but really it would have been more of a shock, since I knew her, if she had kept it.

Across the pond the fisherman shifted his fishing pole to his left hand, its string arching gently with no fish on it yet. He used his right hand to brush back his dark hair, then unzipped his jeans and began to move his arm rhythmically.

I turned on my video camera and eased away from the rock. Hide me, I prayed. The fisherman's back stayed turned to me. Janine rounded the shore into the last light before the storm and came within camera shot. Her head was down as if it had been forced there. Where was Julia? Where was Katie? I didn't dare look away from the camera to try to spot them. I knew better than to leave and go for help. But I wanted it; I wanted help. I wanted my mother and Mrs. Gagnon and Mr. Gagnon and the mill lady. I wanted the cops.

☺ *Janine*

When I saw the fisherman arrive, I began to go a little nuts. Something lit red and angry in me. I didn't care if he *was* a good sign, he and his bass fishing. I wanted him to go away and stay there. And I wasn't going to put up with wondering what he'd do to Kathleen, to Katie, to Marcy, to me.

"I'm going to see what that man is fishing for," I told Marcy sharply. Her head snapped up when she heard my voice, and

I could see that she thought my tone was meant for her. There was that familiar disappointment in her eyes. Oh, well, I told myself, I can't explain it to her, and I can't help it. I don't want her to come with me; I want to handle this myself.

I said meanly, "Stay here, will you?"

Her net dropped onto the surface of the water, and she lifted it up in her fist as if she'd like to throw it in my face.

"I'll be back later," I said.

"Why bother?" asked Marcy, shaking her head.

He wasn't fishing the mouth of the stream today but the deep place where the pond met high cattails along the far side. I made my way along the shallow edge to the stream and crossed it carefully, keeping my eyes on my feet.

The rocks along the edge of the pond were smooth and steady under my bare feet. Before long they gave way to smaller stones that rolled around and slowed my progress.

I glanced back at Marcy in time to see her disappear up the steps to the millhouse. The fisherman and I were alone, he on one side and I on the other, and I was closing the gap between us. Had he seen me yet?

The sky was growing dark beyond the rock bluff, but not so dark that I couldn't tell the exact moment that the fisherman saw me or the precise second when he moved his hand to the zipper of his jeans. I kept walking, although my back and my knees felt as wobbly as the stones. At the foot of the bluff, where the stones become pebbles, I felt my feet sink, and I stopped. Then I lifted my head and looked across the little space—as narrow as the road between our house and the Gooches'—that separated me from the fisherman.

◗ *Eric*

Janine stopped just ten feet away from the fisherman. She began to talk, standing there with her bare feet in the sand, her face like thunder, raindrops falling. I've never heard anybody sound the way she sounded: furious, agonized, hell-bent on changing the world by hollering. At first it was swearing. I had to wonder where she learned it because it was as bad as anything I'd heard at Haycock, and that was an accomplishment.

As her voice rose, the words came clearer. "What kind of person are you? What do you think you're *doing*? You don't *do* that here! You *can't* do that here! This isn't *your* place. It's everybody's. People can't worry about coming here because they'll have to see you like that! This place belongs to the *fish*! It's *their* pond! It's not your place to do this! And *I'm not your person to do it to*!"

My breath was coming in gasps, but I kept on taping. She was hoarse now, screaming, at the end of her rope.

"I'm my own person!" she bellowed. "I'm *mine*! So just *get out of here*!"

He was going. He was zipping up his pants and gathering up his gear. Then he changed his mind and took a step toward her, dropping his fishing pole onto the sand.

That's when I took the camera away from my eye and leaped to my feet. "Janine!" I shouted. "Janine!" As Janine looked up and the man whirled to see me high on the bluff behind him, Julia burst over the crest of the hill, sped past me, and went flying down the side of the hill too fast to fall, flying at the fisherman, screaming, "Get away from my sister!"

The fisherman took off running with Julia in pursuit, and Janine and I stood there, she on the beach, I on the bluff, absurdly paralyzed. Janine was crying out loud now, sobbing, still yelling after him, and I was stuck with my godforsaken broken leg at the top of the bluff. If I moved, I couldn't watch the van, to see if he made it there ahead of Julia, and in that instant three things happened: I wondered where Katie was. And I saw flashing blue and red lights coming along our road. And Janine began to call my name.

I gave up worrying about my leg and followed Julia's route down the bluff by sliding on my rear, camera and all. I got to Janine at last, had my arm around her, and made her sit on the cold sand, and I held on to her as if she were Katie to keep her from going after the man and Julia or doing anything else amazing. "The police are there," I said, and she stopped crying and sat staring at the rain falling on the pond and over us and around us.

"Good fishing weather," she said, and I thought maybe she was in shock, something I'd heard about but didn't know what it was.

I was aware of some kind of commotion going on beyond the bluff, but I just concentrated on Janine. She took the camera into her lap and sat clutching it, her evidence.

"You probably wouldn't want to look at that tape," I said, "but you would be proud of yourself if you did."

"I wasn't brave," she said after a while. "I was stupid. He might have— I shouldn't have—" She stopped, breathing hard. "What good did it do?" she asked seriously.

It was hard to hug her and shake her at the same time, but that's what I did. In her lap the video camera whirred, running down its battery.

"Everybody hates me," she whispered. It sounded like the kind of thing Katie would say in a bad, selfish mood, but Janine really meant it.

"No," I said.

She nodded. "It's worse than that. They all think I hate them."

"I don't think that," I said. You can't look at somebody the way I've looked at Janine, the way I've observed her, the way I've seen her, and come out on the wrong side of her.

"So you've got a big, ugly mouth sometimes," I admitted, "but it looks like it came in handy."

She sighed a long, shuddering sigh full of tears and fear and exhaustion. Then, again, she surprised me.

"You can say that again." She laughed. "You can say that again, Ee-rack."

Then it seemed like everybody on Kingfisher Lane or Henry Street had converged on this little spot of water and woods. Janine's father drove his pickup truck right up to the pond as though he owned the place, leaped out, and picked Janine up as if she were Katie's size, right up off the ground, and held her. Her mother arrived in time to put her arms around both of them, and around Jeff and Julia, too. They stood there in a big knot of people, and that's when I got up off the sand and went to look for Katie.

But before I had walked two steps, my mother was in front of me.

"What is all this?" she said, holding me by the shoulders. "What's been happening? And where's your sister?"

"Eric!" It was Charlie, on the other side of the pond, standing behind Katie with his hands on her shoulders. Marcy and the mill lady were with them. They began walking toward us, around the edge, and Mom and I went to meet them, and along the way I tried to tell Mom.

"This man was— Janine was— He— They—" To my surprise, there were tears rolling down my cheeks.

Mom stopped me, right there by the pond, with Charlie walking along slowly toward me. "It's all right," she said, startled. "Whatever it is, it's over."

Now I felt I had to console Mom. "He didn't touch her," I said.

"But was he going to?"

I nodded.

"Oh, Eric," she said. "And you—"

"I got it," I said, looking down at my camera, which I'd been lugging along, unnoticed, in my arms. "I got it all on video."

Katie, spooked by the police cars, threw herself at Mom and me together. Charlie was still straggling along behind her.

"Wait there!" he called. "I'll come to you." I stood still and just breathed.

He came up to me at last and looked at my face. "Marcy said you ran down that hill," he said. "Your leg must be hurting."

"Oh, Eric," my mother said.

Whatever shock I was in burned off right then, and my leg started hurting as if it had been broken yesterday.

JANINE

SCIENCE OBSERVATION

MAY 21

I got rid of the fisherman who was going to ruin my whole summer at the wetlands. When I went around the pond toward him, Marcy had gone inside to Kathleen.

Together they looked out the window, and Marcy says Kathleen almost had a heart attack, and called the police. But Jeff had already done that.

In the end just about everybody in the whole neighborhood, both Kingfisher Lane and Henry Street, was at the wetlands. Seeing them all, and thinking what had happened to me, and what could have happened to me, I wanted to run home alone, up the stairs to the bathroom across the hall from my room, and throw up, just throw up.

It was Eric who sat with me on the sand, Eric who wouldn't leave me alone there, Eric who told me I was brave when I wanted to roll up into a ball and sink to the bottom of the pond like a fish egg.

They wouldn't let me go: to my house or the bathroom or the bottom of the pond. The police needed my statement for their records. I wouldn't talk. I couldn't speak. It was Eric who took his video camera out of my lap and held it up. "Here's what happened," he said to them all. "See for yourselves what happened and what Janine did. I've got it all on video."

Chapter 12

*T*he way Charlie Panucci describes her, thinks Artie O'Halloran, Janine has turned over a new leaf pretty much overnight. Something about turning in a criminal, although there was something kind of sexy involved, too, or so he has heard. He doesn't care. If other people want to like her, that cuts down the pressure on him. On the baseball field she's fine, but everywhere else—what a dweeb!

Panucci is a sap sometimes, the way he has to like every-body, just everybody. Since he can't play baseball this season, it seems he just wants to hang out with those kids at his bus stop: the kid with the broken leg and that serious tall girl, Marcy what's-her-name, and her, the Gag.

She still plays baseball as well as ever, luckily. The team is 6 and 2 on the season, not bad. He fields a line drive, flips the ball over to her. She stomps on second base to make the out and throws to first. That's still the same, anyway. What else matters?

☺ Janine

Once it was all over, you would have thought I was back in kindergarten, the way my parents treated me. They wanted to stand with me at the bus stop. I refused. Eric would be there, after all. But he wasn't because he wasn't going to school, because his leg was sore from sliding down the bluff and he had to go to the doctor. Daddy wanted to drive me to school or to have Julia do it, but I said no.

I wanted to get it over with. I was going to have to look all the kids in the eye sooner or later. It would be easier to do it in stages, starting with Henry Street, than to step out of the car in front of school and confront everyone at once. So, for the first time in eight years, I let my father drive me around the corner to Charlie Panucci's bus stop.

Marcy was there, and when she saw me, she came walking to meet me. I couldn't smile. My face felt stuck together. But Marcy only said, "Are you going to Kathleen's after school? She asked me to ask you."

"Why not?" I said. "You don't think I'm chicken, do you?"

She just smiled and shook her head no. "Anyway, he's gone," she said. "Because of you."

Then Charlie came out of his house. He was walking a bit stiffly, and he looked pale, but his black hair and brown eyes were the same as always. I walked right over to him. "Are you all right?" I demanded.

He raised his right elbow a little and laid his left hand on the right side of his chest. "I'm a little stiff here, but otherwise—"

"I'm glad you're all right," I interrupted. There was nothing left to say, so I turned away and stood to the side, afraid to be with anybody.

But Charlie moved closer and said, "Some of the guys are going to say things."

"What things?" said Marcy, coming to stand at my side. The younger kids—Charlie's fifth-grade brother and his little friends—started listening, too.

"Stupid things," said Charlie. "About that fisherman. You know."

My chin came up then.

"They're nervous, that's all," Charlie went on. "People say mean things sometimes when they're worried."

Who exactly was he talking about?

"They can say whatever they want!" I sputtered. "I—"

Marcy said, "It's just because they're scared. They're afraid they might get hurt sometime, too." She wasn't nosy; she was concerned.

Charlie said, "But underneath they're glad you're all right." The bus was coming down the street. The kids were all looking at me with sympathetic, curious, kind eyes. I put my backpack on both shoulders and took my time about adjusting the straps. I didn't want to meet any of those eyes.

Tomorrow I would go back to my own bus stop, now that I'd said what I needed to say to Charlie. It didn't matter whether Eric was there or not. My parents would just have to turn me loose. It wouldn't take long; they always had before.

I climbed on the bus behind Marcy and sat three seats away. When she saw where I'd gone, she got up and moved to the seat right in front of me.

"I want to ask you something," she said. Then, not waiting for an answer, not caring, she went on. "Do you think Eric Gooch would let you borrow his camera? The frog eggs are changing so fast. I think it would be great to get them on video."

SCIENCE OBSERVATION
MAY 22

Mr. Lincoln: By now you know all about what happened at the pond, from the newspapers and everything, if not from good old word of mouth. I don't know if I can bear to watch Janine anymore after this. Maybe I'll switch to observing myself, the way she did. But I wouldn't be as interesting. And I could never be as brave. I just wanted to let you know that I learned a lot from watching her.

JANINE

SCIENCE OBSERVATION
MAY 23

Mr. Lincoln, thank you for your note. I'm okay now.

I'm turning in this newspaper article as an objective description of what happened at the wetlands this week. You can see that my second subject, Kathleen Moreno, is good in a crisis.

I don't think the reporter has very good observational

skills. I know she couldn't use my name, since I'm a minor, but she could have called me something more than "slight." And Julia says "spirited" is not exactly the word to describe me. When it comes to swearing, she says, the word for me is "inspired." It's all right there on Gooch's tape; his video has audio.

▶ *Eric*

It was a week after the arrest and five days after the X rays showed that I hadn't done myself any real harm scrambling down the bluff to Janine. I had just come home from school and was getting started on my last observation for Mr. Lincoln when the doorbell rang. I was quicker getting to the door than I had been for a long time.

There was more gray in my father's light brown hair, without a doubt. He looked thinner, which made him look fashionable, in contrast with Mom in the jeans and T-shirt she wears every minute that she's not trying to sell houses. He was also browner. He'd picked up a tan somewhere.

None of the questions in my head made the connection to my mouth. Then my mother emerged from the kitchen, grabbed my father by the elbow as though she'd been expecting him, and said to me, "Give us half an hour, Eric."

I stalked up to the roof, still stunned, and kept an eye on my watch while I took some readings: 72° Fahrenheit. Partly cloudy. Chance of afternoon showers. And Lionel's car was in the Gagnons' driveway.

The mood was kind of indefinable when I went back downstairs. "Here he comes, the conquering hero," announced my mother, trying to lighten things up. I tried to gauge what was happening by her eyes but saw only that she had her guard up against Dad.

"I'm not a hero, Mom," I said quietly. She'd been saying a lot of that kind of junk since two days ago, and I was tired of it. It was Janine who was the brave one.

My father stood up and shook my hand, something he has never done before. How old do you have to be—or how separated—before your father stops kissing your cheek and starts shaking your hand? The fact is, I was feeling pretty ancient as it was, and a hug would have felt good right then.

My mother got up and went to the refrigerator, started pouring milk and getting out peanut butter, and I sat down beside my father.

"Eric," he said after a few minutes of small talk about my leg and school and what time Katie's bus came, "I'm proud you've finally trained your camera on something other than the sky. I hear now you're stopping crime."

He pulled a little camera out of his pocket, a nice little 35mm camera, the kind that fits right into the palm of your hand and takes great still pictures. It had a built-in flash and a little telephoto lens. I sat holding it and looking at it and still couldn't find anything to say except thank you. What I wished I could say was: "Four months away, and you bring me a camera?"

Suddenly Katie was home, bursting in the door, leaping into my father's arms, wrapping her arms around him. He cracked his second smile—the first had come when I arrived—but this one seemed even more strained. He'd brought her an aquarium, the kind Mom said we couldn't afford.

Soon Katie and I were sitting at the kitchen table, close

enough so our arms were touching, and Mom and Dad were saying words that shouldn't have surprised either of us by that time. Shouldn't have but did, and Katie and I couldn't help it, we sat there and cried.

They were getting divorced. It would be final by Christmas. Katie and I would spend two weeks with Dad at his new place in Colorado, after school ended, then come back home for the summer. In the fall, once financial support was arranged, I'd go back to Haycock.

"No," I said.

My mother stopped and stared at me. "Eric," she said, "this is hard enough without—"

"I'm not," I said. "I'm not some object you guys can just move around."

"I know that," Mom said. "Your father knows that. But we've agreed—"

"*You've* agreed? Well, I haven't."

"Eric," Dad said, sounding tired, and I didn't even notice, until I thought about it later, that he'd called me by my given name. "You're the same person you've always been. You're the person who's going to go to Haycock Senior School in the fall and get himself a real education. And then on to a real college." As far as my parents were concerned, all the decisions were made. There was nothing to argue about or consider. Dad had spoken. Just like always.

"I have been getting a real education this spring," I shot back. "Marsh Park is good enough for everybody I know, and it's good enough for me."

"Good enough?" my father said in a snotty way. " 'Good enough' is not what I want for you, Eric."

"Well, what about what I want for myself? How do you know I don't like it here? How do you know what I've learned in this school? I've hardly even talked to you all spring."

Mom started to talk, but I was on my feet and not done saying all I had to say. "Where've you been, anyway, Dad, huh?" I said in my hardest voice. All the feelings I'd felt all spring were filling up my chest as I spoke. "Where were you when I was in a cast right up to my hip? Where were you when it was time for spring term at Haycock to start?"

"Eric, listen to me," he said. "A separation is just what it says. You don't get on the phone every day." He acted as if he was conducting a business meeting. My head was about to explode. Or my chest. Or me.

"You listen to me!" I yelled. "This is where I want to be, not away at school. There is a good school here. I have great teachers. I like our house. I like our neighborhood. This is where I want to be, Dad, here, with Mom and Katie. Think about that!"

I'll never believe I had the nerve to walk out on my father, Eric John Gooch, Jr., but I did. Eric John Gooch III had spoken.

✑ Janine

It was the last week of school, and it was hot.

Eric hadn't told anybody but Charlie, Marcy, and me that he wasn't coming back to our school next fall. But he brought his video camera to school so he could make sure he caught everybody for the memories, "such as they are," he said.

He got Charlie showing off his burn scar at recess. He got me hitting a home run when they let us out on the baseball field to get "a breath of fresh air" at noon. He got Kelly Kim, hot and heaving from running (wow), in the cafeteria after the break. And he got Susan and Barbara singing "One more day till vacation." He got Mr. Mitchell Lincoln handing out report cards—I got a B+ in Whole Learning—wearing a stovepipe hat and his cowboy boots.

And, in the evening of the last day of school, he came over with Katie to videotape Marcy's middle-school graduation party in her backyard. It was when the rest of the class went inside to watch the school video that Eric put the little camera in my hand. It wasn't wrapped, not even a ribbon. He said, "It's a gift, but it's not really a present."

"Same thing, Gooch," I said.

"No," he said, "because it was a gift to me. I'm just passing it on."

"*You're* giving me a camera?"

E R I C

Final Assignment: On the basis of your observations, what conclusions can you draw about your subject?

JUNE 9

Mr. Lincoln: If you'd told me at the beginning of this term that Janine Gagnon would wind up being my friend, I would have said you were crazy. If you'd suggested that I'd miss her, I'd have spit in your eye.

Someday maybe I'll let Janine in on my own little secret, my own green science notebook with all my observations about her. For now I'll keep it to myself, knowing what nobody else knows: that nobody could have seen what I saw.

They're going to make me go back to Haycock. I guess you heard that. I kicked and screamed and begged, but it seems like a done thing. I don't have to stay over, though. I can be a day student. Mom's going to drive me for the first two years, and when I'm sixteen, maybe I can buy some kind of secondhand car. Not boarding will save money, my mother says. But that's not why I'm living at home.

I'll miss this class, Mr. Lincoln. But I tell myself that high school would be different, anyway.

I'll try to stay in touch. Maybe Janine and Charlie and Marcy and I can still be friends, even though we're in separate schools. If there's one thing I've learned from studying meteorology, it's that seeing something from a distance can make all the difference.

▶ *Eric*

My video camera was tucked firmly under my arm. "Well, I have this. That's all I really need."

"You don't *need* it at all," Janine said. "Did you ever think of looking through your own eyes?"

Janine was as outspoken as ever. She was trying to get along now, though, have people like her, show if she liked them—and I think, mostly, she really did. It couldn't have been easy, after all those years of being mean. Maybe that's why I wanted to give her the camera so much: to give her her own eye on the world, as well as something to hide behind sometimes when she needed to see but not be seen.

"Do you want to go back to Haycock?" Janine asked me. She was looking through her camera, focusing on Marcy, who was showing Charlie the stakes her father had pounded in the yard where a pool was going to be.

"It's not my choice," I said. "But it's no surprise. At least I get to live at home."

"A half-and-half deal," said Janine.

"Kind of," I said. And I looked at her out of the corner of my eye and bragged, "Katie and I are going to Colorado to see my father, and then I'm going to wilderness college for two weeks in August."

"What happened to golf camp?"

"You ought to go to golf camp," I said. "You'd be good at it." Janine made just the kind of ugly face I expected. I shrugged and tried to sound casual. "So Katie and I will be here, hanging around the neighborhood."

"I wouldn't want to change schools," Janine said hotly. "You ought to fight it."

If only she knew how we'd fought. I had shouted and Mom had yelled and Dad had screamed on the phone and Katie had cried. After a while I got quiet and made a deal. Haycock in the daytime, I said. But not at night. I wanted to be home then, here, not at Haycock. They'd given in. I'd stay here, all year long and almost all summer long. No more cast, and the Morenos were putting in a pool.

"They're liking the video," I said, to change the subject.

You could hear howls coming from inside Marcy's house.

"It's 'cause they're all in love with themselves." Janine snickered.

☺ *Janine*

It was a nice little camera, and I'd already used it to take ten pictures that night, including a sneak shot of Eric doing the bunny hop with Charlie, cane, scabby chest, and all.

Just looking through my new camera, I could understand how seeing the world through a lens might make me a better observer. Through this camera I was constantly zeroing in on the most important part of any scene: the way Charlie's sweet look got even sweeter when he talked to Marcy, Katie doing "I can't pay the rent" with Ee-rack, the stupid look Artie got on his face when he was talking to Susan Hackman, the way Kelly followed Barbara around, looking afraid she would lose her, the way Barbara wished she *could* lose Kelly. You could tell a lot about what might happen, just by watching people. I had a feeling things would get even more interesting in high school, Gooch or no Gooch.

As for my end-of-year prediction, I planned to continue my own observations of Kathleen, although I didn't have to keep on writing things down. Eric was going to video tadpoles for Marcy and me, and this little camera he gave me would come in handy for some other observations I had in mind.

Of course the Gooch had no idea that I knew who he had observed all spring term. I'd known it since the very first day I carried his backpack on the bus. He'd thought I was sitting apart from him just to be snotty. No, it was to get information. Right then and there, while he was struggling up the steps and into a seat, I lifted the cover of his science notebook and cracked it open to the first page, where—in very tiny, scrawly letters—I recognized my own name.

Someday I'd get my hands on his notebook and find out what he'd been observing ever since the beginning of spring term. Then again, maybe I already knew—enough for now, anyway. Sometime, when I was over there baby-sitting Katie or just hanging out, I might sneak up to the Gooch's room and search out that notebook. He was just dweebish enough to leave it where I could find it.

Through the little telephoto lens I watched as Barbara Finney stood up and walked toward me, growing larger and larger, and then—blur!—she put her hand over the camera.

"Do you see what I see?" she asked.

"All I see is your big paw!"

"My mother had my baby book out last night," she said. "There's a picture of you and me on the first day of kindergarten."

"No way," I said.

She looked away, at Kelly approaching, following her as usual, and said, "Yes way."

"Kelly?" I said. "Will you take our picture?" I handed her the camera and stood next to Barbara. Kelly held the camera up to her eye. Click.

*J*anine passes Marcy her little camera and poses with the tiny frog held securely in her hand. It's just a picture for posterity, she tells herself, to help herself remember the frogs they raised from egghood. But the fact is, she chose to release the frog right beside the cattails. Now she won't have *to look away from that spot anymore and remember what happened to her there. Instead, she'll remember the frog.*

"Smile, froggy!" Marcy clicks the shutter. Janine bends to the water's surface, lets her hands float there, then opens them. The little frog is still at first, then kicks its new legs out behind it. They watch for a while, then turn away and walk back along the shore.